THE BOOK OF BALLADS

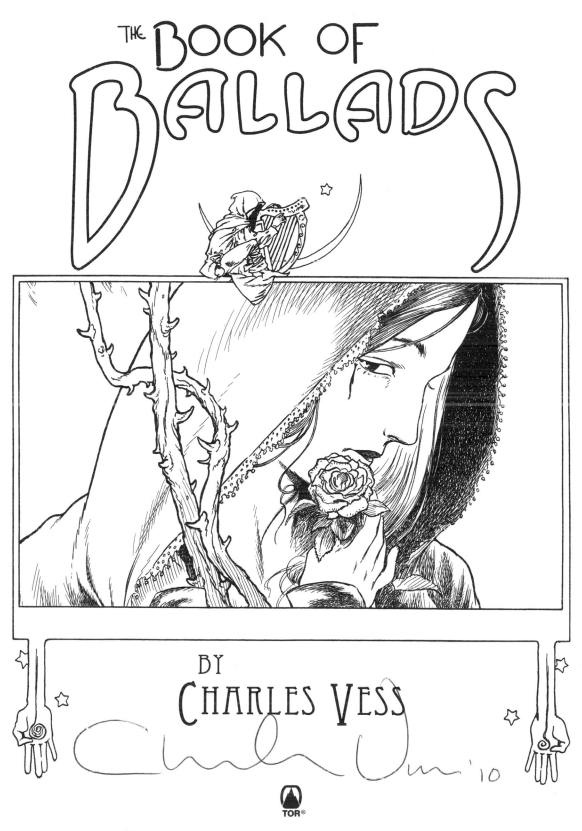

THE BOOK OF BALLADS

BY CHARLES VESS

TOR®

A TOM DOHERTY ASSOCIATES BOOK · NEW YORK

THE BOOK OF BALLADS

Edited by Teresa Nielsen Hayden

A Tor Book
Published by Tom Doherty Associates, LLC
175 Fifth Avenue
New York, NY 10010

www.tor.com

Tor® is a registered trademark of Tom Doherty Associates, LLC.

ISBN 0-765-31214-X
EAN 978-0765-31214-3

First Edition: November 2004

Printed in the United States of America

0 9 8 7 6 5 4 3 2 1

DEDICATION

TO

Jacqui McShee, Sandy Denny, and Maddy Prior,
whose singing first brought these old songs
to vivid life for me

AND TO

all those other singers and musicians
that carry on the folk tradition,
I affectionately dedicate this volume.

CHARLES VESS
Abingdon, Virginia
April 2004

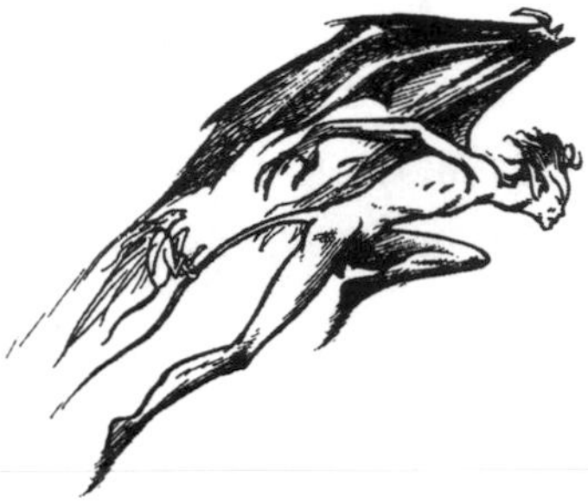

CONTENTS

INTRODUCTION

by Terri Windling

A tale from Scotland's Isle of Skye relates how music first came to those lands. A poor youth found a strange instrument, a triangular harp, floating in the waves. He fished it out, set it upright, and the wind began to play the strings—an eerie, lovely sound the likes of which had never been heard. The boy could not duplicate the sound, although he tried for many long days. So obsessed did he become that his widowed mother ran to a wizard (a "dubh-sgoilear") to beg him to give her son the skill to play the instrument—or else to quell his desire for it. The dubh-sgoilear offered her this choice: he would take away the boy's desire in exchange for the widow's body, or he'd give him the gift of music in exchange for her mortal soul. She chose the latter and returned home where she found her son plucking beautiful, heavenly music from the strings of the harp. But the boy was horrified to learn the price his mother had paid for his skill. From that moment on, he began to play music so sad that even the birds and fish wept. And that, concludes the tale, is why music is capable of wringing our hearts. Perhaps it's also why so many ancient Scottish songs are sorrowful ones, telling tales of treachery, tragedy, love betrayed, and fortunes lost.

From Ireland comes a story explaining the three types of music found in the repertoire of a traditional musician: songs of merriment, songs of sorrow, and songs of supernatural enchantment. Boand was the wife of the Dagda Mor—a deity of the Tuatha De Danann, the faery race of Ireland. As Boand gave birth to the Dagda's three sons, the Dagda's harper played along to ease the woman's labor. The harp groaned with the intensity of the pain as the woman's first child emerged, and so she named her eldest son Goltrai, the crying music. The music made a merry sound as

Boand's second son was born, and so she named the child Gentrai, the laughing music. At last the final infant emerged to music that was soft and sweet. She called the child Suantri, the sleeping music—which was also the music of dreams and enchantment. These same three strains of music occur in the Anglo-Scots ballad of "King Orfeo," who saves his wife from the faeries by playing three fiddle tunes before their king: the notes of joy, the notes of pain, and the magical faery reel.

In this collection, you'll find all three kinds of stories (of merriment, sorrow, and the supernatural), for each is based on the traditional ballads of England, Scotland, and Ireland, or on the ballads that immigrants from those lands transplanted to America.

What is a ballad? The great folklorist Francis James Child defined what he called the "popular ballad" as a form of ancient folk poetry, composed anonymously within the oral tradition, bearing the clear stamp of the preliterate peoples of the British Isles. Ballads, which are stories in narrative verse, are related to folktales, romances, and sagas, with which they sometimes share themes, plots, and characters (such as Robin Hood). No one knows how old the oldest are. It's believed that they are ancient indeed—and yet we have few historical records of them older than the sixteenth century. Little is known for certain about how the oldest ballads would have been performed—but most likely they were recited, chanted, or sung without instrumentation. Right up to the twentieth century, ballads were traditionally sung a cappella, although today it is common to hear them accompanied by harp, guitar, fiddle, and other instruments.

Why do we have so few historical records? Because until relatively recently, they weren't considered important enough to write down. With the rise of literacy, the songs and poems of Britian's great oral tradition began to fall out of favor—and ballads that had once been popular among all classes of society were now deemed primitive, pagan, the province of unlettered country folk. Because of this, few attempts were made to preserve ballads prior to the seventeenth century, and thus many were lost or were passed down through the years in fragmentary form. In the eighteenth century, ballad collection was still haphazard and sporadic, and the fruits of such labor were little regarded in academic circles. Universities did not yet consider folklore a respectable area of study, so manuscript collections remained in private hands, easily lost and forgotten.

In 1765, Bishop Thomas Percy came across one manuscript full of fine old ballads being used to light a kitchen fire. He saved them from the flames and published them in his book, *Reliques of Ancient English Poetry*. Percy's book was a great success. It was much admired by such English Romantic writers as Coleridge, Southey, Shelley, and Keats, as well as German Romantics like Goethe, Tieck, and Novalis, and sparked much literary interest in the songs and legends of bygone days. Another fan of Percy's book was the novelist Sir Walter Scott, who collected the ballads of his native Scotland in the early nineteenth century. Scott sat at the center of a circle of poets and antiquarians who were devotees (and romanticizers) of the ancient history of the British Isles. This group did much to popularize the old songs and tales of Scotland, England, and Ireland—but still no British university would sponsor a proper academic collection of the country's ballads.

That job fell to an American scholar, Francis James Child of Harvard University, who was urged to take on the subject by his frustrated British colleagues. Child hesitated, somewhat daunted by the immensity of the job at hand, and then he plunged in, devoting the rest of his life to the study of ballads. Beginning in the 1870s, Child set out to track down every extant version of every genuine popular ballad in the English and Scottish traditions. He limited himself to England and Scotland becaues the ballads of these countries overlapped, whereas Irish ballads were a separate tradition, requiring a depth of knowledge of Ireland's language and history he didn't possess. His goal was to publish the collected ballads with notes tracing their histories, relating them to songs and tales to be found in folklore the world over. The result of this remarkable labor was *The English and Scottish Popular Ballads,* published in five volumes between 1882 and 1898. It's a work that's still widely used today, revered by scholars and musicians alike.

The life of the man behind these famous books is as interesting as the ballads he loved. Born the son of a sailmaker, Child grew up on the docks of Boston harbor—until his aptitude for learning brought him to the attention of a distinguished Cambridge scholar. The boy was encouraged to transfer from his working-class school to Boston's Latin School, after which he was sponsored at Harvard, where he graduated at the top of his class. Except for two years of study abroad, Child spent the rest of his life at Harvard, rising to become the first chairman of the newly created department of English. He built his substantial reputation on groundbreaking studies of Chaucer and Spenser, but he also had an abiding love for philology, ancient poetry, folklore, and fairy tales. The latter interests had been whetted during the two years Child spent in Germany, where he'd been exposed to the work of the folklore enthusiasts of the Heidelberg Circle of scholars, which included folk song collectors Clemens Brentano and Achim von Arnim, and the remarkable Brothers Grimm. *The English and Scottish Popular Ballads,* noted Child's friend and colleague G. L. Kittredge, "may even, in a very real sense, be regarded as the fruit of these years in Germany. Throughout his life he kept pictures of Wilhelm and Jacob Grimm on the mantel over his study fireplace."

Child was a textual scholar rather than a field collector, and he put his massive ballad compilation together by seeking out every manuscript copy of ballad material he could lay his hands on, with the help of a small army of fellow scholars searching out songs and fragments of songs throughout the British Isles. Another reason he depended on manuscripts rather than the memories of folk musicians was that the British popular ballad, in his view, was no longer a living tradition. The ballads he sought were the ancient ones—not the "broadside ballads" that dominated the nineteenth-century folk musician's repertoire. Broadsheet ballads were authored song lyrics designed to fit traditional tunes, cheaply printed and sold for pennies on street corners from the sixteenth century onward. These were contemporary compositions, rather than ancient poetry from the oral tradition—though sometimes broadside ballads mimicked the language of much older songs, and determining which was which was a problem Professor Child was both intrigued and vexed by. To the dismay of this meticulous scholar, in the absence of clear historical records he was often forced to depend on textual clues and his own best judgment. Fortunately, that judgment was finely honed by his fluency in archaic languages, and his extraordinary knowledge of folklore traditions the world over. He chose, he explained in a letter to a friend, to err on the side of inclusiveness. Where he had lingering doubts about the authenticity of a song variant, he was apt to include it anyway, along with notes outlining his reservations.

His task was greatly complicated by the fact that the ballads of Britain had been so badly recorded and preserved compared with those of other countries such as Denmark. "The ballads should have been collected as early as 1600," he noted sadly; "then there would have been such a nice crop; the aftermath is very weedy." Another complication was that ballads written down and published from the eighteenth century onward had been edited, censored, or "improved" by folklore enthusiasts who were literary men, romantics, rather than rigorous academics. The prime example of this was Percy's famous *Reliques of Ancient English Poetry*. Child and other folklorists suspected that Percy had altered the text of ballads to suit the literary tastes of his day—particularly as Percy would not allow an examination of the ballad manuscript in his possession. Working with British scholar F. J. Furnivall, Child was instrumental in persuading Percy's descendants to finally release this manuscript, which did indeed confirm that Percy had edited and "improved" the original ballads.

Sifting through the mountain of material he collected, sniffing out alterations and forgeries, Child amassed a group of 305 songs with their roots in the oral tradition, along with variants of each song, sometimes in dozens of alternate versions. The final volume of *The English and Scottish Popular Ballads* was completed the year of Child's death, but he died before writing the book's introduction, which would have explained his method of selection and given us an overview of his work. Yet even without this, *The English and Scottish Popular Ballads* was hailed by critics on both sides of the Atlantic and became a cornerstone of modern folklore scholarship. In addition, Child was instrumental in establishing the American Folklore Society, serving as its first president from 1888 to 1889. But sadly, Child did not live to see that movement flower in subsequent years, and he died doubting his work had relevance to a modern age. "If he'd lived just a little longer," says Mark F. Heiman of Loomis House, which published a handsome new edition of *The English and Scottish Popular Ballads,* "he would have seen the golden age of the ballad collector and folklorist. He would have seen how important his life's work really was."[1]

Child's work went on to inspire a whole new generation of folklorists, men and women who weren't quite so convinced that the oral tradition was irretrievably dead and gone. One of them was Cecil Sharp, who began collecting English folk songs and dance tunes in the early years of the twentieth century. Sharp was a trained musician, and unlike Child he was also interested in preserving the music of the ballad tradition, rather than viewing ballads primarily as poetry. He noted that the Child ballads were rarely part of the repertoire of the elderly singers he listened to in the countryside; they'd been replaced by broadside ballads and other more recent songs. Sharp wondered if the older ballads might have survived among the British and Scottish settlers in America, particularly among the descendants of settlers in isolated mountain regions, where "pennysheets" of modern ballads would not have been available.

Between 1914 and 1918, Sharp made two extensive trips through the Appalachian Mountains, collecting over a thousand songs with the aid of his secretary, Maud Karpeles. Sharp and Karpeles discovered that many of the Child ballads were indeed still known and performed in Appalachia, although sometimes the titles and lyrics had changed somewhat in this new setting. Sharp published these ballads in his now-classic *English Folk Songs from the Southern Appalachians,* which in turn inspired new folklore studies and new collection efforts throughout the United States.

Despite the keen interest of folklorists, ballads remained a specialized interest

1. Quoted in "Child's Garden of Verses," by Scott Alarik, *Sing Out!,* Vol. 46, #4.

for much of the twentieth century, until the huge folk music revival of the 1960s and '70s. In those years, Joan Baez, Judy Collins, and other singers recorded ballads from the Child collections, and a Celtic music revival exploded across the British Isles, Brittany, and America. Folk-rock bands like Pentangle, Fairport Convention, and Steeleye Span updated the ballads for a new generation, while singers like Martin Carthy, Frankie Armstrong, and June Tabor created an audience for traditional music played in more traditional ways. Thirty years later, the revival is still going strong, and Child ballads are still being sung by performers like Niamh Parsons, Kate Rusby, Loreena McKennitt, and many others. (See the Discography Notes at the back of this book for specific recommendations.)

In the 1970s, while musicians were rediscovering and reinventing the genre of folk music, writers were rediscovering and reinventing the genre of fantasy fiction. The audience for both of these things overlapped. It's not hard to understand why. Fantasy writers often work with themes that hark back to the oral tradition—to folktales, myths, and sagas steeped in the lore of our folk heritage. A number of writers who came to the fantasy genre in the 1970s and '80s were also folk musicians or singers (such as Ellen Kushner, Charles de Lint, Emma Bull, and Jane Yolen) and music permeated their books. Charles de Lint's *The Little Country*, for example, is set among folk musicians in Cornwall. Emma Bull's *War for the Oaks* concerns folk-rock musicians in '80s-era Minneapolis. Jane Yolen wove original ballads into *Sister Light, Sister Dark* and its sequels. Ellen Kushner retold a classic ballad in her novel *Thomas the Rhymer*, and created an anthology of magical stories about music, *The Horns of Elfland*. A number of other fiction writers also turned to ballads for inspiration, fleshing out the bare bones of song narratives to turn them into stories and novels. One need only dip at random into the pages of *The English and Scottish Popular Ballads* to discover why this material would appeal to writers of magical fiction. There you'll find stories not told in *Ballads*, like "Kemp Owyne," in which a young woman is turned into a loathsome dragon. Knight after knight comes to slay the beast. The dragon kills them all in turn, with tears of regret on her scaly cheeks. It is only when a knight puts down his sword and kisses her horrible face that the spell is broken and the dragon turns back into a beautiful maiden.

In "The Elfin Knight," a girl hears faery music and longs for a supernatural lover. The elf knight appears at her request, but gives her one look and tells her she's too young. The song becomes a riddling song (similar to "Parsley, Sage, Rosemary and Thyme")—though this is a riddling match that is charged with distinctly sexual overtones.

In "Reynardine," a mysterious man seduces a woman as she walks among the hills. The man is a shapechanger, a were-fox. We don't know what he will do to her in the castle where he steals her away, but our last image of Reynardine is of his sharp teeth gleaming brightly in the twilight.

In "Clark Sanders," seven brothers stand over their sleeping sister and her lover, discussing what they should do to this knight who has stained the family honor. Six of them agree that they should leave the sleeping couple alone, but the seventh takes out his sword and runs it through the sleeping man's heart. When the young woman wakes, she finds her love is a bloody corpse beside her. She goes mad with grief, the song ends . . . and then the story is taken up again in another ballad, called "Sweet William's Ghost." The spirit of the murdered man returns to the girl's window. She begs him to kiss her, but he will not: "My mouth it is full cold, Margaret, / It has the smell now of the ground; / And if I kiss thy comely mouth, / Thy days will not be long."

This idea that the dead may not touch the living is echoed in "The Unquiet Grave." A maiden sits in a cemetery for twelve months, mourning her lover. Finally the spirit appears and asks, in a rather irritated manner, "Who sits here crying and will not let me sleep?" The maiden begs it for one kiss, but she is refused by the revenant: "O lily, lily are my lips; / My breath comes earthy strong, / If you have one kiss of my clay-cold mouth, / Your time will not be long."

Not all ballads in the British folk tradition concern magic, faery, or the supernatural. Other common themes are love (usually tragic), death (usually gruesome), and family troubles that make the soap operas of our own age pale by comparison: "What is that blood on your sword, my son, what is that blood, my dear-o? It's the blood of my sister, Mother, who I have killed in the greenwood-o. . . ." (In this song, the brother is trying to avoid discovery of the fact that he's made his sister pregnant.)

"What I like best about ballads," says fantasy writer Delia Sherman, "is that they're plots with all the motivations left out. Why did Young Randall's stepmother want to poison him? Why choose eels? Why did Randall eat them (especially if they were green and yellow)? There's a novel there, or at least a short story. Ballads give you classic human situations, and also some decidedly unclassic ones, exploring relationships between lovers, parents, and children, between friends, masters, and servants. Many of them deal with power and powerlessness, which is one of the central themes of fairy tales, too; but it seems to me that ballads are more pragmatic, more realistic, in their denouements. Not every villain gets his/her just deserts. I can imagine a ballad variant of 'Beauty and the Beast' in which Beauty comes too late and sings a plaintive last verse over the Beast's body, about how she will sew him a shroud of the linen fine and sit barefoot in the dark all her days, for the love of him she loved too late."

Of all of the ballads recounted by Child, "Tam-Lin" has captured the imagination of more fiction writers than any other single ballad, perhaps because of its sensual theme and unusual hero: an independent, courageous, stubborn young woman, pregnant with her woodland lover's child, determined to save him from the Faery Queen and the unearthly Faery Court. Elizabeth Marie Pope's fine novel *The Perilous Gard* sets the tale in the courts of Elizabethan Scotland, while Pamela Dean's *Tam Lin* uses the ballad as the basis of a contemporary coming-of-age tale set among the theater students at a 1960s-era college campus. Patricia A. McKillip's *Winter Rose* is a gorgeous novel that weaves "Tam-Lin" with a second faery ballad called "Thomas the Rhymer," setting this wintry romance in a land reminiscent of medieval England. Alan Garner's *Red Shift* is a subtle, powerful reworking of the ballad's themes. Dahlov Ipcar makes interesting use of the ballad in her short novel *A Dark Horn Blowing,* and Joan Vinge retells the ballad straightforwardly in her story "Tam-Lin."[2] Diana Wynne Jones, like Patricia McKillip, combines the tale with "Thomas the Rhymer" in her novel *Fire and Hemlock,* setting her mysterious tale among classical musicians in modern-day England. In addition to these, Liz Lochhead's long, wry poem "Tam-Lin's Lady"[3] is well worth seeking out, as is Jane Yolen's picture book *Tam Lin,* illustrated by Charles Mikolaycak.

"Thomas the Rhymer"—the story of a Scottish musician who kisses the Queen of Elfland and then is bound to her service for seven long years—is another popular tale among fantasy writers and readers. In addition to the excellent McKillip and Wynne Jones books listed above, the ballad inspired Bruce Glassco's unusual short story "True Thomas,"[4] and is spendidly retold in Ellen Kushner's award-winning novel *Thomas the Rhymer.*

> I had to do Thomas [Ellen recalls] because, like every other writer, I knew Thomas was my story. He holds the mythic power of King Arthur in the hearts of poets: the artist who is literally seduced by his muse, comes closer to her than any human should to the source of his art, and is profoundly changed. He can never be at home in this world again, and yet he must continue to live in it. That's how every writer feels, I think.

2. Published in *Imaginary Lands,* edited by Robin McKinley.

3. Published in *The Grimm Sisters* and *Dreaming Frankenstein,* by Liz Lochhead.

4. Published in *Black Swan, White Raven,* edited by Ellen Datlow and Terri Windling.

Many writer friends had talked about writing a Thomas story someday, kind of like an actor playing King Lear: it's a Great Subject that probably should not be tackled in one's youth. I still feel a little humble about it. I don't think I've written the definitive Thomas; I've just written my Thomas, the Thomas who addressed issues that were upon me in those years. Twenty years from now, I might like to do him again.

Ellen's *Thomas the Rhymer* also draws upon the Child ballads "The Trees They Do Grow High" and "The Famous Flower of Serving Men." The latter is the story of a woman whose husband, a knight, is murdered by her own mother. The heroine dons men's clothes and goes to court, where the king soon falls in love with her—while the murdered knight returns as a white dove shedding blood-red tears through the forest. Delia Sherman used this ballad as the basis of her thought-provoking novel *Through a Brazen Mirror*. "I heard Martin Carthy's version of 'Famous Flower,'" says Delia, "and it haunted me with questions. If a mother so hated her child, why not just kill her and be done? Perhaps there was more to it than simple hatred. Another question prompted by the ballad had to do with the role of cross-dressing in a medieval culture. A third question could be stated as this: In all these ballads with girls dressed as boys, the man falls in love with the boy, not the girl. What would happen if he wasn't relieved to discover his beloved's true sex? In short, 'Famous Flower' gave me a beautiful, mysterious narrative framework upon which to hang all my favorite concerns: gender confusion, different kinds of love, the single-mindedness of the mad, foundlings and their origins."

Patricia C. Wrede's "Cruel Sisters"[5] and Gregory Frost's "The Harp That Sang"[6] are both memorable tales based on "Cruel Sister" (aka "Twa Sisters"), the ghostly story of a murdered girl and a harp made out of bone. Midori Snyder's "Alison Gross"[7] is based on the ballad of that title about a man changed to an ugly worm when he spurns the kisses of a witch. A number of works draw upon "The Grey Selchie," a poignant ballad of love and shape-shifting—including Jane Yolen's "The Grey Selchie,"[8] Laurie J. Marks's "How the Ocean Loved Margie,"[9] and Paul Brandon's evocative, music-filled novel *Swim the Moon*. Greer Ilene Gilman's *Moonwise* is a fever-dream of a novel brimming with Celtic balladry from every corner of

5. Published in *Book of Enchantments*, by Patricia C. Wrede.
6. Published in *Swan Sister*, edited by Ellen Datlow and Terri Windling.
7. Published in *Life on the Border*, edited by Terri Windling.
8. Published in *Neptune Rising*, by Jane Yolen.
9. Available on line at: http://www.endicoot-studio.com/jMA04summer/rrOceanLovedMargic.html

the British Isles; Gilman has an extensive knowledge of the folk tradition and uses it to unique effect. *Ghostriders, The Songcatcher, The Ballad of Frankie Silver, The Rosewood Casket, She Walks These Hills, The Hangman's Beautiful Daughter,* and *If I Never Return Pretty Peggy-o* are magical mystery novels by Sharyn McCrumb that use the themes of traditional ballads from the southeastern mountains of America.

Artist Charles Vess has listened to and loved old ballads for more than twenty-five years. "They are great stories," he says, "filled with exactly the things I love to draw best: magic, adventure, romance, suspense, historical settings, the lands of Faerie, and supernatural creatures that range from beautiful to hideous." In 1994, Charles conceived the idea of illustrating a series of comics based on traditional folk ballads. He spoke with a number of ballad-loving writers who promised him scripts for the new series, which began with a story by Charles de Lint retelling "Sovay." The series was published by Green Man Press, the small press Charles runs with his wife, Karen Shaffer, in Bristol, Virginia. In Europe, it was published by Phoenix [Italy] and Bull Dog [France]. The book you hold in your hands collects all of the original Green Man Press ballads, along with four additional ones: "Alison Gross" (reprinted from *The Forbidden Book*), "The Black Fox" (reprinted from *Firebirds,* an anthology edited by Sharyn November), and two brand-new tales, "The Great Selchie of Sule Skerry" and "The Three Lovers."

The thirteen tales that follow provide an excellent introduction to traditional ballads for readers not yet familiar with them. Readers who *are* familiar with them also have a treat in store. We hope that this book will lead readers to seek out the many excellent recordings of ballads available today—and to this end, Ken Roseman has provided a thorough discography at the end of the volume.

In an article on Francis James Child published in *Sing Out!* magazine, Scott Alarik asked folk musician Martin Carthy (one of the greatest modern interpreters of Child ballads) why people should still be singing these ancient ballads today. For the same reasons they sang them long ago, says Carthy, "because they're fabulous stories; because they tell you immense amounts about people and how they treat each other, trick each other, cheat and chisel and love each other. There's an extraordinary understanding of humanity in them."

He goes on to say, "You do have to sometimes kick the buggers into life, find them a tune, give the lyrics a kick here and there. And they can take it; they're fabulously resilient. I really do believe there's nothing you can do to these songs that will hurt them—except for not singing them."

Charles Vess and the writers in these pages have done a wonderful job of taking these old ballads and "kicking the buggers into life." Singing is one way to keep ballads alive. And this book is another.

Further Reading

The English and Scottish Popular Ballads, edited by Francis James Child.

The Singing Tradition of Child's Popular Ballads, edited by Betrand Harris Bronson.

Bishop Percy's Folio Manuscript, Ballads and Romances, edited by John W. Hales and Frederick J. Furnivall.

Medieval Lyric: Middle English Lyrics, Ballads, and Carols, edited by John C. Hirsh.

English Folk Songs from the Southern Appalachians, edited by Cecil James Sharp.

"Child's Garden of Verses: The Life Work of Francis James Child," by Scott Alarik, *Sing Out!* Vol. 46, #4.

Earth, Air, Fire, Water: Pre-Christian and Pagan Elements in British Songs, Rhymes, and Ballads, by Robin Skelton and Margaret Blackwood.

"WHERE ARE YOU GOING?"
SAID THE FALSE KNIGHT ON THE ROAD.

"I AM GOING TO THE SCHOOL,"
SAID THE WEE BOY, AND STILL HE STOOD.

"WHAT IS THAT UPON YOUR BACK?"
SAID THE FALSE KNIGHT ON THE ROAD.

"TO BE SURE, IT IS MY SCHOOL BOOKS,"
SAID THE WEE BOY, AND STILL HE STOOD.

"WHAT'S THAT YOU'VE GOT IN YOUR HAND?"
SAID THE FALSE KNIGHT ON THE ROAD.

"PEAT FOR THE SCHOOL FIRE."
SAID THE WEE BOY, AND STILL HE STOOD.

"WHOSE ARE THOSE SHEEP?"
SAID THE FALSE KNIGHT ON THE ROAD.

"THEY ARE MINE AND MY MOTHER'S."
SAID THE WEE BOY, AND STILL HE STOOD.

"HOW MANY OF THEM ARE MINE?"
SAID THE FALSE KNIGHT ON THE ROAD.

"ALL THOSE THAT HAVE BLUE TAILS."
SAID THE WEE BOY, AND STILL HE STOOD.

"I WISH YOU WERE IN THAT TREE."
SAID THE FALSE KNIGHT ON THE ROAD.

"AND A GOOD LADDER UNDER ME."
SAID THE WEE BOY, AND STILL HE STOOD.

"AND THE LADDER FOR TO BREAK,"
SAID THE FALSE KNIGHT ON THE ROAD,

"AND YOU TO FALL DOWN,"
SAID THE WEE BOY, AND STILL HE STOOD.

"I WISH YOU WERE IN THE SEA,"
SAID THE FALSE KNIGHT ON THE ROAD.

"AND A GOOD BOAT UNDER ME,"
SAID THE WEE BOY, AND STILL HE STOOD.

"AND THE SHIP FOR TO BREAK,"
SAID THE FALSE KNIGHT ON THE ROAD.

"AND **YOU** TO BE DROWNED,"
SAID THE WEE BOY, AND STILL HE STOOD.

"I WISH YOU WERE IN THE WELL,"
SAID THE FALSE KNIGHT ON THE ROAD.

"AND YOU THAT DEEP IN HELL,"
SAID THE WEE BOY, AND STILL HE STOOD.

·END·

THE FALSE KNIGHT ON THE ROAD

"O, where are you going?"
    Quoth the false knight upon the road.
"I'm going to my school,"
    Quoth the wee boy, and still he stood.

"What is that upon your back?"
    Quoth the false knight upon the road.
"Truly it is my books,"
    Quoth the wee boy, and still he stood.

"Who owns those sheep?"
    Quoth the false knight upon the road.
"They're mine and my mother's,"
    Quoth the wee boy, and still he stood.

"How many of them are mine?"
    Quoth the false knight upon the road.
"All those that have blue tails,"
    Quoth the wee boy, and still he stood.

"I wish you were in yonder tree,"
    Quoth the false knight upon the road.
"And a good ladder under me,"
    Quoth the wee boy, and still he stood.

"And the ladder for to break,"
    Quoth the false knight upon the road.
"And you for to fall down,"
    Quoth the wee boy, and still he stood.

"I wish you were in yonder sea,"
    Quoth the false knight upon the road.
"And a good ship under me,"
    Quoth the wee boy, and still he stood.

"And the ship for to break,"
    Quoth the false knight upon the road.
"And you to be drowned,"
    Quoth the wee boy, and still he stood.

"I wish you were in yonder well,"
    Quoth the false knight upon the road.
"And you that deep in hell,"
    Quoth the wee boy, and still he stood.

KING HENRY

Let never a man a-wooing wend
That lacketh thingis three:
A store of gold, an open heart,
And full of charity.

And this I speak of King Henry
When he lay burd alone,
For he's taken him to a haunted hall
Seven miles from the town.

He's chased the deer down him before
And the doe down by the glen,
Till the fattest buck in all the flock
King Henry he has slain.

His huntsmen followed him to the hall
To make them burly cheer,
When loud the wind was heard to howl
And an earthquake rocked the floor.

As darkness covered all the hall
Where they sat at their meat,
The grey dogs, yowling, left their food
And crept to Henry's feet.

And louder howled the rising wind
And burst the fastened door,
When in there came a grisly ghost
Stamping on the floor.

Her head hit the rooftree of the house,
Her middle you could not span.
Each frightened huntsman fled the hall
And left the King alone.

Her teeth were like the tether-stakes
Her nose like club or maul,
And nothing less she seemed to be
Than a fiend that comes from hell.

"Some meat, some meat, you King
    Henry,
  Some meat you bring to me."
"And what meat's in this house, lady,
  That I'm to give to ye?"
"Oh, you go kill your berry-brown
    steed,
  And bring some meat to me."

And he has slain his berry-brown steed,
It made his heart full sore,
For she's eaten it up, both skin and
    bone,
  Left nothing but hide and hair.

"More meat, more meat, you King
    Henry,
  More meat you give to me."
"And what meat's in this house, lady,
  That I'm to give to ye?"
"Oh, you must kill your good
    greyhounds,
  And bring some meat to me."

And he has slain his good
    greyhounds,
It made his heart full sore,
For she's eaten them up, both skin and
    bone,
  Left nothing but hide and hair.

"More meat, more meat, you King Henry,
 More meat you give to me."
"And what meat's in this house, lady,
 That I'm to give to ye?"
"Oh, you must slay your good goshawks,
 And bring some meat to me."

And he has slain his good goshawks,
It made his heart full sore,
For she's eaten them up, both skin and
    bone,
Left nothing but feathers bare.

"Some drink, some drink, you King
    Henry,
 Some drink you give to me."
"And what drink's in this house, lady,
 That I'm to give to ye?"
"Oh, you sew up your horse's hide,
 And bring some drink to me."

And he's sewn up the bloody hide
And a pipe of wine put in,
And she's drank it up all in one gulp,
Left never a drop therein.

"A bed, a bed, now, King Henry,
 A bed you'll make for me.
 Oh, you must pull the heather green
 And make it soft for me."

And he has pulled the heather green
And made for her a bed,
And taken has he his good mantle,
And over it he has spread.

"Take off your clothes now, King Henry,
 And lie down by my side."
"Oh, God forbid," said King Henry,
"That ever the like betide;
 That ever a fiend that comes from hell
 Should stretch down by my side."

When the night was gone, and the day
    was come
And the sun shone through the hall,
The fairest lady that ever was seen
Lay betwixt him and the wall.

"Oh, well is me!" said King Henry,
"How long will this last with me?"
 Then out and spoke that fair lady,
"Even till the day you die."

"For I've met with many a gentle knight
 That gave me such a fill,
 But never before with a courteous knight
 That gave me all my will."

THOMAS the RHYMER

True Thomas lay on Huntlie bank,
A ferlie[1] he spied wi'his e'e,[2]
And there he saw a lady bright
Come riding doon by Eildon Tree.

Her skirt was o' the grass-green silk,
Her mantle o' the velvet fyne,
At ilka[3] tett[4] of her horse's mane
Hung fifty siller[5] bells and nine.

True Thomas he pulled aff his cap
And louted[6] low down to his knee:
"All hail, thou mighty Queen of Heaven!
For thy peer on earth I never did see."

"O no, O no, Thomas," she said,
"That name does not belong to me;
I am but the queen of fair Elfland
That am hither come to visit thee."

"Harp and carp,[7] Thomas," she said,
"Harp and carp along wi' me,
And is ye dour[8] to kiss my lips,
Sure of your body I will be."

"Betide me weel, betide me woe,
That weird[9] shall never daunton me;"
Syne he has kissed her rosy lips,
All underneath the Eildon Tree.

"Now ye maun[10] gang wi' me," she said,
"True Thomas, ye maun gang wi' me,
And ye maun serve me seven years,
Thro' weel and woe, as may chance to be."

She mounted on her milk-white steed,
She's ta'en[11] True Thomas up behind,
And aye[12] whene'er her bridle rung
The steed flew faster than the wind.

O they rode on, and farther on—
The steed gaed[13] swifter than the wind—
Until they reached a desert wide,
And living land was left behind.

"Light down, light down now, True
    Thomas,
And lean your head upon my knee;
Abide and rest a little space,
And I will show you ferlies three,

"O see ye not yon narrow road,
So thick beset with thorns and briars?
That is the path of righteousness,
Tho' after it but few enquires,

"And see ye not that braid, braid road
That lies across that lily leven[14]?
That is the path of wickedness,
Tho' some call it the road to heaven.

"And see ye not that bonny road
  That winds about the fernie brae[15]?
  That is the road to fair Elfland
  Where thou and I this night maun gae.

"But, Thomas, ye maun hold your tongue,
  Whatever ye may hear or see,
  For if you speak work in Elflyn land
  Ye'll ne'er get back to your ain countrie."

Syne they cam' to a garden green,
  And she pu'd[16] an apple frae a tree;
  "Tak' this for thy wages, True Thomas,
  It will gi' ye the tongue that can never lie."

"My tongue is mine ain,"[17] True Thomas
  said,
"A guidly[18] gift ye wad[19] gie to me!
  I neither dought[20] to buy or sell,
  At fair or tryst where I may be.

"I dought neither speak to prince or peer,
  Nor ask of grace from fair ladye."
"Now hold thy peace," the lady said,
"For as I say, so must it be!"

He has gotten a coat o' the even cloth,[21]
  And a pair of shoon[22] of velvet green,
  And till seven years were gane and past
  True Thomas on earth was never seen.

1 a wondrous thing	12 every time
2 eye	13 went
3 every	14 flower-covered lawn
4 lock	15 fern-covered hillside
5 silver	16 pulled
6 bowed	17 own
7 recite (as a minstrel)	18 goodly
8 dare	19 would
9 fate, destiny	20 could, was able
10 must	21 fine cloth
11 taken	22 shoes

T'WAS EARLY IN THE SPRING WHEN ALL THE BUDS WERE SWELLING, THAT WILLIAM CAME FROM HIS OWN COUNTRY, AND HE COURTED BARBARA ALLEN.

·BARBARA ALLEN·
©MIDORI SNYDER AND CHARLES VESS·96

"MY HEART WAS GLAD AND FREE AND I TARRIED THERE TO LET HIM KISS ME, NOT THINKING AT ALL OF SORROW. HIS ARMS WERE STRONG, BUT HIS LIPS ON MINE WERE COLD..."

"IT WAS IN THE GLEN WHERE FIRST I MET WILLIAM, MORE HANDSOME THAN ANY OF OUR YOUNG MEN. HIS EYES LIKE THE SLOES AND HIS VOICE SWEET AS THE THRUSH."

"AS I SLEPT ONE DAY BESIDE A STREAM, I WAS SEDUCED BY A LEANAN-SIDHE. THE FAIRY CREATURE BOUND ME TO HER, TAKING HALF MY SOUL."

"I HUNGER FOR WHAT HAS BEEN TAKEN FROM ME, SO I MUST STEAL WHAT I CAN FROM A WOMAN'S MOUTH AND A WOMAN'S BODY."

IS THERE NO WAY TO BREAK SUCH A CURSE?

BUT NEVER ONCE HAVE I BEEN DENIED!

ONLY IF I AM DENIED. THEN WILL MY DEATH FOLLOW...

AND THE RELEASE OF MY SOUL.

BARBARA ALLEN

It being late all in the year
The green leaves they were falling,
When young William rose from his own
    country
Fell in love with Barbara Allen.

"Get up, get up," her mother says,
"Get up and go and see him."
"Oh Mother dear, do you not mind the
    time
That you told me how to slight him."

"Get up, get up," her father says,
"Get up and go and see him."
"Oh Father dear, do you not mind the
    time
That you told me how to shun him."

Slowly, slowly she got up,
And slowly she drew nigh him.
Slowly she went to his bedside
And slowly looks upon him.

"You're lying low, young man," she says,
"And almost near a-dying."
"One word from you would bring me to
If you be Barbara Allen."

"One word from me you never will get,
Nor any young man breathing.
The better of me you never will be
Though your heart's blood was a-spilling."

"Look down, look down at my bed foot,
It's there you'll find them lying.
Bloody shirts and bloody sheets,
I wept them for you, Allen.

"Look up, look up at my bed head.
It's there you'll find them hanging.
My gold watch and my gold chain,
I bestow them to you, Allen."

As she was going home to her father's
    hall,
She heard the death bell ringing.
And every clap that the death bell gave
Was "Woe be to you, Allen."

As she was going home to her mother's
    hall,
She saw the funeral coming.
"Lay down, lay down that weary corpse,
Till I get looking on him."

She lifted the lid up off of the corpse
And bursted out with laughing.
And all his weary friends around
Cried, "Hard-hearted Allen."

She went into her mother's house.
"Make my bed long and narrow.
For the death bell did ring for my true
    love today,
It'll ring for me tomorrow."

Out of one grave there grew a red rose.
Out of the other a briar.
And they both twisted into a true lovers'
    knot
And there remain forever.

"OH MOTHER, OH MOTHER, COME UNRIDDLE THIS SPORT,
UNRIDDLE IT ALL AS ONE,
AS TO WHETHER I SHOULD MARRY FAIR ELLENDER
OR GO BRING THE BROWN GIRL HOME?"

MOTHER, WHAT AM I TO DO?

SINCE YOUR FATHER'S DEATH IN THIS RECENT DISASTROUS WAR, WE ARE RUINED, MY SON. WE HAVE NOTHING. NOTHING! YOU MUST REALIZE THIS AND ACT ACCORDINGLY. OTHERWISE, WE WILL LOSE TINEGAL AND ALL OUR LANDS, WHICH HAVE BEEN IN OUR FAMILY SINCE TIME BEGAN. IT IS UP TO YOU, MY SON.

"THE BROWN GIRL SHE HAS HOUSE AND LAND, FAIR ELLENDER HAS NONE. THEREFORE I ADVISE YOU AS MY ELDEST SON, TO GO AND BRING THE BROWN GIRL HOME."

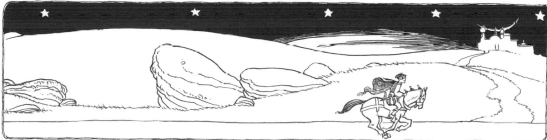

"HE TOOK HER BY THE LILY WHITE HAND,
HE LED HER THROUGH THE HALL,
HE LED HER TO THE HEAD OF THE TABLE
AMONG THE GENTRIES ALL."

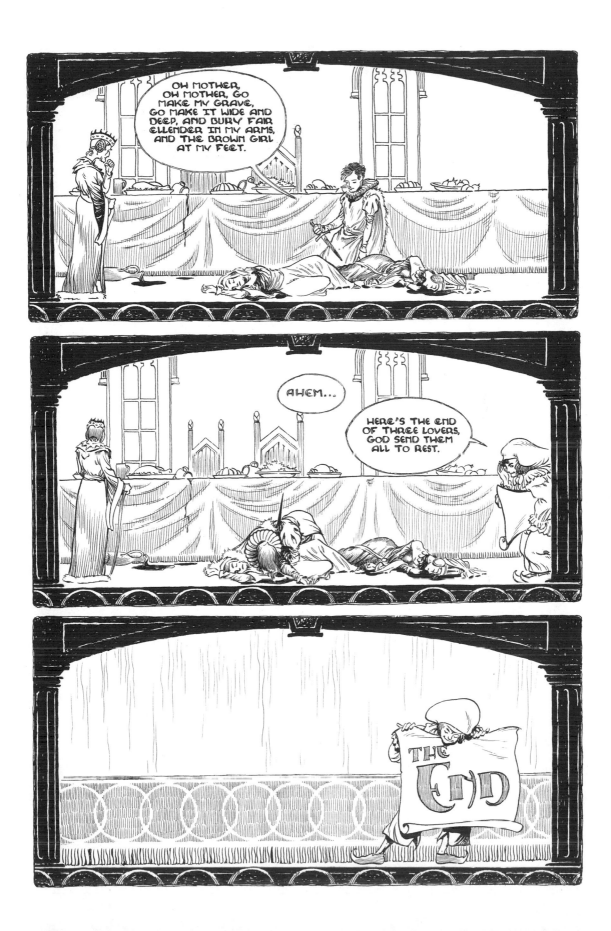

THE THREE LOVERS

Lord Thomas, he was a bold keeper,
The keeper of the king's deer,
Fair Ellender was a fair young lady,
Lord Thomas he loved her dear.

"Oh Mother, oh Mother, come unriddle
    this sport,
Unriddle it all as one,
As to whether I should marry Fair
    Ellender,
Or go bring the brown girl home."

"The brown girl she has house and land,
Fair Ellender has none,
Therefore I advise you as my eldest son,
To go bring the brown girl home."

He rode unto Fair Ellender's house,
He knocked on the door,
There was none so ready as Fair Ellender
    herself,
To rise and ask him in.

"What news, what news, Lord Thomas,"
    she cried,
"What news you bring to me?"
"I've come to ask you to my wedding,
 Is that good news to thee?"

"Bad news, bad news, Lord Thomas,"
    she cried,
"Bad news you bring to me.
 I thought I was to be your bride,
 And you the bridegroom to be."

"Go saddle me up the milk-white horse,
 Go saddle me up the brown,
 Go saddle me up the swiftest horse,
 That ever walked the ground."

She rode unto Lord Thomas' house,
She knocked at the door,
There was none so ready as Lord
    Thomas himself,
To rise and ask her in.

He took her by the lily-white hand,
He led her through the hall,
He led her to the head of the table,
Among the gentries all.

"Is this your bride, Lord Thomas?" she
    cried,
"She looks most wonderful brown,
 When you could 'a' married as fair a
    young lady,
 That ever sun shone on."

The brown girl had a pen knife in her hand,
It was most keen and sharp,
She pierced it through Fair Ellender's side,
And it entered in her heart.

"What is the matter?" Lord Thomas, he cried,
"What is the matter?" cried he,
"Why don't you see my own heart's blood,
Come trickling down by me?"

He took the brown girl by her hand,
He led her through the hall,
He took a sword and cut her head off,
And hurled it against the wall.

"Oh Mother, oh Mother, go make my grave,
Go make it wide and deep,
And bury Fair Ellender in my arms,
And the brown girl at my feet."

He placed the sword against the floor,
The point against his breast,
Saying, "Here's the end of three young lovers,
God send them all to rest."

"O I FORBID YOU MAIDENS ALL,
THAT WEAR GOLD IN YOUR HAIR
TO COME OR GO BY CARTERHAUGH,
FOR YOUNG TAM-LIN IS THERE."

The Setting: Sunset by a small pool under a decaying tower overgrown with weeds. The pool is quartered by four trees: Willow, Holly, Rowan, and Elder. It is Samhain, the end of the Celtic year, 450 B.C.

Tam-Lin (thought): The last my senses drink of earth: the red-gold rays of a dying sun, the heat of a horse beneath me, the first frost on air that startles my naked flesh.

Air is denied me. It is my first death.

Second death . . . taken from earth, tempered in fire . . . death of fierce pain. The knife cut will be deep.

Third will be water. I welcome it . . . and She-of-the-Willow welcomes me, reaching to embrace me as the Elder, Rowan, and Holly tree look on.

I am the chosen . . . the Holy Sacrifice! My blood nourishes, my life makes fertile, and my soul . . . guards this place. For such as me, there is no hope of rebirth!

A thousand years pass by . . .

For more nights and days than mortal could imagine, I serve as the well's guardian, and always I long for the sun on my face . . . the taste of cooked meat . . . the feel of warm flesh against my own.

Then, with one dawning, change comes in the shape of a piper. He loves this spot, and from it makes a set of pipes.

Piper: Many thanks, kind tree. In payment, I'll gift thee with music.

Tam-Lin (thought): The chanter he carves of hornbeam, the rootwood of the Holly, Holy Tree! Each berry a blood-drop from one of its thousand spears! The drones he makes of Rowan . . . red-white branch of immortality . . . and the reeds of Elder fashions . . . tree of doom and of death.

Bellows and bag from the the skin of a stag that has drunk seven years from my well, and its antlers, he works for the mounts.

Piper (smiling): Lovely, now you'll sing the year through, old fellow. . . . not just the autumn!

Setting: The castle hall of Lady Janet's father, somewhere in Scotland.

Tam-Lin (thought): These sacred things the piper chooses . . .
though it is I who guide the choice! When he plays, 'tis my song
that pours from the pipes and my story that falls from his lips!

"O I forbid you, maidens all,
that wear gold in your hair
To come or go by Carterhaugh,
for young Tam-Lin is there . . .
there's none that goes by Carterhaugh
that leave him not a fee,
Either their rings, or green mantles,
Or else their maidenhead!"

Janet: Carterhaugh, it is my own! My Daddie gave it me! So, I'll
come and go by Carterhaugh . . . and ask no leave from thee!

"Janet has kilted her green mantle,
Just a little above the knee,
And she has braided her yellow hair
A little above her bree . . .
Young Janet's away to Carterhaugh,
As fast as she can flee!"

Setting: Carterhaugh, the ancient ruin, rising above the ancient pool.

"When she came to Carterhaugh . . ."

Janet: What's this . . . ? A rose! And the well half-frozen and the sap just in the Willow!

Tam-Lin's spirit arises as mist from the pool and begins to assume a mortal form.

> "She had not pulled a double rose,
> A rose but only two,
> When up and spoke young Tam-Lin crying,
> 'Lady, pull no more.
>
> 'How dare you pull those flowers?
> How dare you break those wands?
> How dare you come to Carterhaugh
> Withouten my command?' "

Janet: Carterhaugh, it is my own! My Daddie gave it to me! And, I will come and go by here . . . without any leave . . . of . . .

> "He's taen her by the milk-white hand
> Among the leaves so green,
> And what they did, I cannot tell,
> The leaves were in between!"

Setting: The castle hall.

> "Four and twenty ladies fair
> Were playing at the chess
> And out then came the fair Janet
> As green as any glass.
> Out then spake her father dear
> His manner meek and mild."

Father: Ever alas, sweet Janet! I fear you go with child!

Janet (firmly): If I go with child, myself must bear the blame! There's not a lord about your house, shall get my bairn's name! If my love were an earthly knight, as he's an elfin grey, I would not give my own true-love for any Lord that you have! The steed that my true-love rides on, is lighter than the wind. With silver he is shod before, with burning gold behind!

"Janet has kilted her green mantle,
Just a little above her knee,
And she has gone to Carterhaugh
For to pull the Scathing tree!"

Tam-Lin: How dare you pull that herb among the leaves so green,
to kill the bonny babe that we got us between!

Janet: You must tell me, Tam-Lin, were you once a mortal knight?

In his effort to regain his mortality Tam-Lin lies to Janet.

"Once it fell upon a day,
A cold day and a snell,
That I was from the hunting come,
And from my horse I fell
The Queen of Fairies caught me
In yon green hill to dwell.
And pleasant is the Fairy land
But, an eerie tale to tell . . .
For at the end of seven years
We pay a tithe to hell!"

Tam-Lin (pleadingly): I am so fair and full o' flesh, I'm feared it be myself!

Janet: What must I do to help you?

Tam-Lin: On Halloween, at the midnight hour, the Fairy Folk do ride.
Those that would their true love win, at Miles Cross must they bide . . .

Janet: But, how shall I know thee, among so many knights?

Tam-Lin: First let pass the black, lady, then let pass the brown, but run up to the milk-white steed, and pull the rider down!

Piper (whispering): Gloomy, gloomy was the night and eerie was the way . . . As fair Janet in her green mantle, to Miles Cross did she go!

Tam-Lin (thought): And, again, it is sunset, at the time of first frost! Again, the gates between life and death will open . . . For sweet Janet will pull the rider down! She will wrestle with beasts and with serpents . . . Accepting the pain of this bringing forth . . .

And knowing that, at pain's end, there is joy!

And me? I will have life! Life!

Tam-Lin: Not for a while, as a man . . . but that will come. In time, it will come! And, what are a few short years, when I have waited for a thousand and then four-score hundred more!

With the touch of icy water, nerves catch fire, lung gulps air, and the scream, harsh death denied me, breaks from my new-born throat!

Naked I am, and human, as she wraps me in green. Once more will I feel the sun on my face . . . feel the warmth of woman's skin against my own . . .

As my own cheek rests on the white breast of my beloved.

TAM-LIN

O I forbid you, maidens a',
    That wear gowd on your hair,
To come or gae by Carterhaugh,
    For young Tam-Lin is there.

There's nane that gaes by Carterhaugh
    But they leave him a wad,
Either their rings, or green mantles,
    Or else their maidenhead.

Janet has kilted her green kirtle
    A little aboon her knee,
And she has broded her yellow hair
    A little aboon her bree,
And she's awa to Carterhaugh,
    As fast as she can hie.

When she came to Carterhaugh
    Tam-Lin was at the well,
And there she fand his steed standing,
    But away was himsel.

She had na pu'd a double rose,
    A rose but only twa,
Till up then started young Tam-Lin,
    Says, "Lady, thou's pu nae mae.

"Why pu's thou the rose, Janet,
    And why breaks thou the wand?
Or why comes thou to Carterhaugh
    Withoutten my command?"

"Carterhaugh, it is my ain,
    My daddie gave it me;
I'll come and gang by Carterhaugh,
    And ask nae leave at thee."

Janet has kilted her green kirtle
    A little aboon her knee,
And she has snooded her yellow hair
    A little aboon her bree,
And she is to her father's ha,
    As fast as she can hie.

Four and twenty ladies fair
    Were playing at the ba,
And out then cam the fair Janet,
    Ance the flower amang them a'.

Four and twenty ladies fair
    Were playing at the chess,
And out then cam the fair Janet,
    As green as onie glass.

Out then spak an auld grey knight,
    Lay oer the castle wa,
And says, "Alas, fair Janet, for thee
    But we'll be blamed a'."

"Haud your tongue, ye auld fac'd knight,
    Some ill death may ye die!
Father my bairn on whom I will,
    I'll father nane on thee."

Out then spak her father dear,
    And he spak meek and mild;
"And ever alas, sweet Janet," he says,
    "I think thou gaes wi child."

"If that I gae wi child, father,
    Mysel maun bear the blame;
There's neer a laird about your ha
    Shall get the bairn's name.

"If my love were an earthly knight,
　　As he's an elfin grey,
I wad na gie my ain true-love
　　For nae lord that ye hae.

"The steed that my true-love rides on
　　Is lighter than the wind;
Wi siller he is shod before,
　　Wi burning gowd behind."

Janet has kilted her green kirtle
　　A little aboon her knee,
And she has snooded her yellow hair
　　A little aboon her bree,
And she's awa to Carterhaugh,
　　As fast as she can hie.

When she cam to Carterhaugh,
　　Tam-Lin was at the well,
And there she fand his steed standing,
　　But away was himsel.

She has na pu'd a double rose,
　　A rose but only twa,
Till up then started young Tam-Lin,
　　Says, "Lady, thou pu's nae mae.

"Why pu's thou the rose, Janet,
　　Amang the groves sae green,
And a' to kill the bonnie babe
　　That we gat us between?"

"O tell me, tell me, Tam-Lin," she says,
　　"For's sake that died on tree,
If eer ye was in holy chapel,
　　Or Christendom did see?"

"Roxbrugh he was my grandfather,
　　Took me with him to bide,
And ance it fell upon a day
　　That wae did me betide.

"And ance it fell upon a day,
　　A cauld day and a snell,
When we were frae the hunting come,
　　That frae my horse I fell;
The Queen o Fairies she caught me,
　　In yon green hill to dwell.

"And pleasant is the fairy land,
　　But, an eerie tale to tell,
Ay at the end of seven years
　　We pay a tiend to hell;
I am sae fair and fu o flesh,
　　I'm feard it be mysel.

"But the night is Halloween, lady,
　　The morn is Hallowday;
Then win me, win me, an ye will,
　　For weel I wat ye may.

"Just at the mirk and midnight hour
　　The fairy folk will ride,
And they that wad their true-love win,
　　At Miles Cross they maun bide."

"But how shall I thee ken, Tam-Lin,
 Or how my true-love know,
Amang sae mony unco knights
 The like I never saw?"

"O first let pass the black, lady,
 And syne let pass the brown,
But quickly run to the milk-white steed,
 Pu ye his rider down.

"For I'll ride on the milk-white steed,
 And ay nearest the town;
Because I was an earthly knight
 They gie me that renown.

"My right hand will be glovd, lady,
 My left hand will be bare,
Cockt up shall my bonnet be,
 And kaimd down shall my hair,
And thae's the takens I gie thee,
 Nae doubt I will be there.

"They'll turn me in your arms, lady,
 Into an esk and adder;
But hold me fast, and fear me not,
 I am your bairn's father.

"They'll turn me to a bear sae grim,
 And then a lion bold;
But hold me fast, and fear me not,
 As ye shall love your child.

"Again they'll turn me in your arms
 To a red-het gaud of airn;
But hold me fast, and fear me not,
 I'll do to you nae harm.

"And last they'll turn me in your arms
 Into the burning gleed;
Then throw me into well water,
 O throw me in wi speed.

"And then I'll be your ain true-love,
 I'll turn a naked knight;
Then cover me wi your green mantle,
 And cover me out o sight."

Gloomy, gloomy was the night,
 And eerie was the way,
As fair Jenny in her green mantle
 To Miles Cross she did gae.

About the middle o the night
She heard the bridles ring;
This lady was as glad at that
As any earthly thing.

First she let the black pass by,
    And syne she let the brown;
But quickly she ran to the milk-white steed,
    And pu'd the rider down.

Sae weel she minded whae he did say,
    And young Tam-Lin did win;
Syne coverd him wi her green mantle,
    As blythe's a bird in spring.

Out then spak the Queen o Fairies,
    Out of a bush o broom:
"Them that has gotten young Tam-Lin
    Has gotten a stately groom."

Out then spak the Queen o Fairies,
    And an angry woman was she:
"Shame betide her ill-far'd face,
    And an ill death may she die,
For she's taen awa the bonniest knight
    In a' my companie.

"But had I kend, Tam-Lin," she says,
    "What now this night I see,
I wad hae taen out thy twa grey een,
    And put in twa een o tree."

"O, WHERE HAVE YOU BEEN, MY LONG-LOST LOVE, THIS SEVEN YEAR AND MORE? I'M COME TO SEEK MY FORMER VOWS YOU PROMISED ME BEFORE."

"O HOLD YOUR TONGUE OF YOUR FORMER VOWS, FOR THEY WILL BREED SAD STRIFE; O HOLD YOUR TONGUE OF YOUR FORMER VOWS, FOR I AM BECOME A WIFE."

WHEN SHE GOT ON THAT GALLANT SHIP,
NO MARINERS COULD SHE BEHOLD,
BUT THE SAILS WERE O' THE TAFFETIE,
AND THE MASTS O' THE BEATEN GOLD.

THEY HAD NOT
SAILED A LEAGUE,
A LEAGUE,
    A LEAGUE BUT
BARELY THREE,
    UNTIL SHE
ESPIED HIS CLO-
VEN FOOT,
    AND SHE WEPT
RIGHT BITTERLY.

HE STRUCK THE TOP-MAST WITH HIS HAND,
THE FORE-MAST WITH HIS KNEE,
HE BROKE THAT GALLANT SHIP IN TWAIN,
AND SANK HER IN THE SEA!

·END·

THE DAEMON LOVER

"Where have you been, my long-lost
    lover,
    This seven long years and more?"
"I've been seeking gold for thee, my love,
    And riches of great store.

"Now I'm come for the vows you
    promised me,
    You promised me long ago."
"My former vows you must forgive,
    For I'm a wedded wife."

"I might have been married to a king's
    daughter,
    Far, far across the sea;
But I refused the crown of gold,
    And it's all for the love of thee."

"If you might have married a king's
    daughter,
    Yourself you have to blame;
For I'm married to a ship's-carpenter,
    And to him I have a son.

"Have you any place to put me in,
    If I with you should gang?"
"I've seven brave ships upon the sea,
    All laden to the brim.

"I'll build my love a bridge of steel,
    All for to help her oer;
Likewise webs of silk down by her side,
    To keep my love from the cold."

She took her only son into her arms,
    And sweetly did him kiss:
"My blessing go with you, and your
    father too,
    For little does he know of this."

As they were walking along the sea-side,
    Where his gallant ship lay in,
So ready was the chair of gold
    To welcome this lady in.

They had not sailed a league, a league,
    A league but scarcely three,
Till altered grew his countenance,
    And raging grew the sea.

When they came to yon sea-side,
    She set her down to rest;
It's then she spied his cloven foot,
    Most bitterly she wept.

"O is it for gold that you do weep?
    Or is it for fear?
Or is it for the man you left behind
    When that you did come here?"

"It is not for gold that I do weep,
    O no, nor yet for fear;
But it is for the son I left behind
    When that I did come here.

"O what a bright, bright hill is yon,
    That shines so clear to see?"
"O it is the hill of heaven," he said,
    "Where you shall never be."

"O what a black, dark hill is yon,
    That looks so dark to me?"
"O it is the hill of hell," he said,
    "Where you and I shall be.

"Would you wish to see the fishes swim
    In the bottom of the sea,
Or wish to see the leaves grow green
    On the banks of Italy?"

"I hope I'll never see the fishes swim
    On the bottom of the sea,
But I hope to see the leaves grow green
    On the banks of Italy."

He took her up to the topmast high,
    To see what she could see;
He sunk the ship in a flash of fire,
    To the bottom of the sea.

"OLD MARKET'S A FUNNY PLACE."

STORY AND ART ©+™ CHARLES DE LINT AND CHARLES VESS '96

Twa Corbies

"IT'S RIGHT DOWNTOWN, BUT WHEN YOU STEP INTO ITS NARROW STREETS IT'S LIKE YOU'VE STEPPED BACK IN TIME, TO AN OLDER, OTHER PLACE."

"THE RHYTHMS ARE DIFFERENT THERE. THE SOUND OF TRAFFIC SEEMS TO DISAPPEAR. THE AIR TASTES CLEANER AND IS FILLED WITH THE SMELL OF BAKING AND FISH, EVEN AT THIS TIME OF NIGHT."

"I LIKE WALKING HERE AT NIGHT WHEN I'VE BEEN IN THE STUDIO TOO LONG. I DON'T EVEN BOTHER TO CHANGE. I JUST GO OUT IN MY PAINT-STAINED CLOTHES, THE SCENT OF MY TURPS AND LINSEED TRAILING ALONG BEHIND ME."

"BUT THERE'S NO ONE TO SMELL THEM."

"AT THIS TIME OF NIGHT, ALL THE CAFES IN OLD MARKET ARE CLOSED UP AND EXCEPT FOR THE ODD CAT, EVERYBODY'S IN BED..."

"OR CHECKING OUT THE NIGHTLIFE DOWNTOWN."

"OR ALMOST EVERYBODY."

"AND THEN THE CORBIES CAME FOR THEIR DINNER AND WHAT BAUBLES THEY COULD FIND."

THAT'S US. WE WERE THE CORBIES. DID WE EAT YOU?

WHAT SORT OF BAUBLES?

YOU MEAN LIKE THIS?

TWA CORBIES

As I was walking all alone,
I heard two corbies making their moan,
The one unto the other did say,
"Where shall we go and dine this day?

"In behind yon old turf dyke,
I wot there lies a new-slain knight,
And nobody knows that he lies there
But his hawk and his hound and his lady fair.

"His hound is to the hunting gone,
His hawk to fetch the wild-fowl home,
His lady's ta'en another mate,
So we may make our dinner sweet.

"You'll sit on his white neck-bone,
And I'll pick out his bonny blue e'en;
With one lock of his golden hair
We'll thatch our nest when it grows bare.

"Many a one for him makes moan,
But none shall know where he is gone;
O'er his white bones, when they are bare,
The wind shall blow for evermair."

HE MAKES GOOD TIME.

"SOVAY, SOVAY, ALL ON A DAY,
SHE DRESSED HERSELF IN MAN'S ARRAY,
PUT A BRACE OF PISTOLS ALL AT HER SIDE,

"TO MEET HER TRUE LOVE,
TO MEET HER TRUE LOVE,
AWAY SHE DID RIDE."

WHAT'S THIS I SEE?

DOES ANOTHER MEAN TO
TEST WILLIE'S COURAGE AS I
WOULD TEST HIS LOVE?

THIS I WON'T ALLOW.

HE KNOWS THE FIRST SHOT WILL FELL THE MOUNT HE'S RAISED FROM A COLT.

"HE DELIVERED UP HIS GOLD
            IN STORE.
AND STILL SHE CRAVED FOR
            WANTING MORE.
THAT DIAMOND RING THAT I
            SEE YOU WEAR:
O HAND IT OVER.
O HAND IT OVER AND YOUR
            LIFE I'LL SPARE.

"FROM MY DIAMOND RING
            I WOULD NOT PART.
FOR IT'S A TOKEN FROM MY
            SWEETHEART.
SHOOT AND BE DAMNED, YOU
            ROGUE, SAID HE.
AND YOU'LL BE HANGED,
AND YOU'LL BE HANGED THEN
            FOR MURDERING ME."

SOVAY

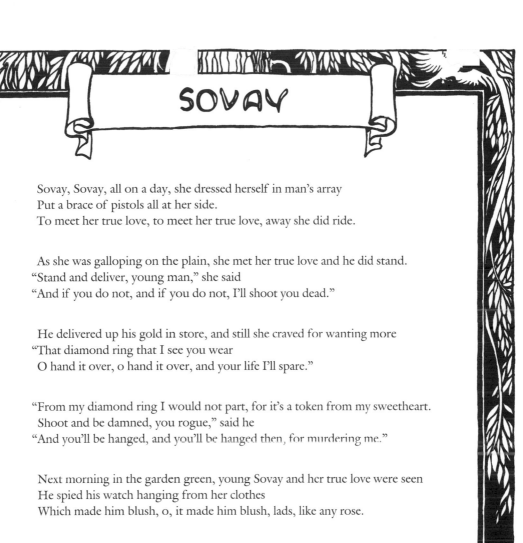

Sovay, Sovay, all on a day, she dressed herself in man's array
Put a brace of pistols all at her side.
To meet her true love, to meet her true love, away she did ride.

As she was galloping on the plain, she met her true love and he did stand.
"Stand and deliver, young man," she said
"And if you do not, and if you do not, I'll shoot you dead."

He delivered up his gold in store, and still she craved for wanting more
"That diamond ring that I see you wear
O hand it over, o hand it over, and your life I'll spare."

"From my diamond ring I would not part, for it's a token from my sweetheart.
Shoot and be damned, you rogue," said he
"And you'll be hanged, and you'll be hanged then, for murdering me."

Next morning in the garden green, young Sovay and her true love were seen
He spied his watch hanging from her clothes
Which made him blush, o, it made him blush, lads, like any rose.

"Why do you blush you silly young thing? I thought to have that diamond ring:
'Twas I who robbed you of all on that plain.
So here's your gold, love, here's your gold, and your watch and your chain.

"I only did it for to know, if you would be a man or no
If you'd given me that ring," she said.
"I'd have pulled the trigger, pulled the trigger and shot you dead."

THE GALTEE FARMER

Oh there was an old Galtee farmer and he had an old Galtee mare
He brought her to Enniscorthy, boys, to sell her at the fair
Said the son all to the father, "I'll do the best I can
The price of her is twenty guineas, but look, I'll take one pound."

Up comes a Dublin buyer: "For to bid I am inclined
The price of her is twenty guineas, but look, I'll give one pound."
So quickly then he paid for her before time look around
And he went into a stable and he pulled her in behind,
Put a saddle and a bridle and a jockey all on her back.
You would swear she was a racer after coming off the track.

Says the son all to the father, "There's a mare for sale close by
She looks so bright and handsome and enticing to my eye."
She looks so bright and handsome and the jockey turned around,
Said, "The price of her is fifty guineas, but look, I'll take five pounds."

Said the son all to the father, "Now be quick and make up your mind.
The price of her is fifty guineas, but look, he'll take five pounds."
So quickly then they paid for her and away from the fair they went
And as they jogged along the road they were both well content.

When they came to the little cottage at the bottom of the lane
Who should run to meet them but the little daughter Jane
"Mamma, mamma, here comes the lads, but the mare they did not sell.
But they've hogged her mane and docked her tail
    but you'd know her old jog well."

"Oh what did you get that mare clipped for? She looks so thin and old.
What did you get that mare clipped for. She'll surely catch a cold.
I'll sit down at the table and I'll let my temper cool.
I've been married to you these forty years and you're only a born fool."

©CHARLES VESS

O ALISON GROSS that lives in yon tower,
    The ugliest witch in the north country,
Has trysted me one day up to her bower,
    And many fair speeches she made to me.

Sʜᴇ stroked my head and she combed my hair,
    And she set me down softly on her knee;
Says, "If you will be my lover so true,
    So many fine things I will give to thee."

She showed me a mantle of red scarlet,
    With golden flowers and fringes fine;
Says, "If you will be my sweetheart so true,
    This goodly gift it shall be thine."

"Away, away, you ugly old witch,
    Hold far away and let me be!
I never will be your lover so true,
    And I wish I were out of your company."

SHE brought a shirt of the softest silk,
    Well wrought with pearls about the band;
Says, "If you will be my sweetheart so true,
    This goodly gift you shall command."

She showed me a cup of the good red gold,
    Well set with jewels so fair to see;
Says, "If you will be my sweetheart so true,
    This goodly gift I will give to thee."

"Away, away, you ugly old witch,
    Hold far away and let me be!
I would not kiss your ugly mouth,
    For all the gold in the north country."

SHE'S turned her right and round about,
 And thrice she blew on a grass-green horn;
And she swore by the moon and the stars above,
 That she'd make me rue the day I was born.

Then out she has taken a silver wand,
 And she's turned herself three times round and round;
She muttered such words that my strength it failed,
 And I fell down senseless on the ground.

SHE'S turned me into an ugly worm,
    And made me twine about the tree;
And aye, on every Saturday night,
    Alison Gross came to me.

With silver basin and silver comb,
    To comb my head upon her knee;
But ere that I'd kiss her ugly mouth,
    I'd sooner go twining around the tree.

BUT as it fell out, on last Hallowe'en,
    When the Fairy Court came riding by,
The Queen lighted down on a flowery bank,
    Close by the tree where I was wont to lie.

She took me up in her milk-white hand,
    And she's stroked me three times over her knee.
She changed me again to my proper shape,
    And no more shall I twine about the tree.

ALISON GROSS

Oh, Alison Gross, that lives in yon tower,
The ugliest witch in the north country,
Has trysted me one day up in her bower,
And many fair speech she made to me.

She stroked my head and she combed my
    hair,
And she set me down softly on her knee;
Says, "If you will be my lover so true,
So many good things I would give to
    you."

She showed me a mantle of red scarlet,
With golden flowers and fringes fine,
Says, "If you will be my lover so true,
This goodly gift it shall be thine."

"Away, away, you ugly witch,
Hold far away and let me be!
I never will be your lover so true,
And I wish I were out of your company."

She next brought a shirt of the softest
    silk,
Well wrought with pearls about the band;
Says, "If you will be my lover so true,
This goodly gift you shall command."

She showed me a cup of the good red
    gold,
Well set with jewels so fair to see
Says, "If you will be my lover so true
This goodly gift I will give to thee."

"Away, away, you ugly witch,
Hold far away and let me be!
I'd never once kiss your ugly mouth
For all the gifts that you could give."

She's turned her right and round about
And thrice she blew on a grass-green
    horn;
She swore by the moon and the stars
    above
That she'd make me rue the day I was
    born.

Then out she has taken a silver wand
And turned her three times round and
    round.
She's muttered such words till my
    strength it did fail,
And she's turned me into an ugly worm.

THE BLACK FOX

An Apologetic Introduction

Sometime around the middle of the 1980s I heard "The Black Fox" on a recording by the North Carolina folk duo, the Pratie Heads. I fell madly in love with it, of course. There was no songwriter credited, and the lyrics had that wonderful feeling of having been polished by centuries down to their essentials that all good old ballads have. So I thought its origins were lost in the mists of time.

Thanks to the Internet, I've learned differently. "The Black Fox" was written by Sheffield songwriter Graham Pratt, based on a fragment of a Yorkshire folktale. You might say the song is proof that the ballad tradition is very much alive, and still an inspiration to writers, artists, and musicians everywhere. More information on Graham and Eileen Pratt and their recordings is available at http://www.folkmusic.net/grahamandeileenpratt/.

Their CDs *Borders of the Ocean* (1997), *Early Birds* (1999), and *Bandstand with Regal Slip* (1999) are available from The Listening Post at http://www.folkmusic.net/catalog/. Their earlier recordings on vinyl include *Clear Air of the Day* (1978/88), *To Friend and Foe* (1980), *Bandstand* (1981), and *Hieroglyphics* (1985).

—Emma Bull

The Black Fox
by Graham Pratt

As we were out a-hunting
One morning in the spring
Both hounds and horses running well
Made the hills and valleys ring

But to our great misfortune
No fox could there be found
And the huntsmen cursed and swore but still
No fox moved over the ground

Up spoke our master huntsman
At the head of hounds rode he
"Well, we have ridden for a full three
  hours
But no fox have we seen

"And there is strength still in me
And I will have my chase
And if only the Devil himself come by
We'd run him such a race"

And then there sprang like lightning
A fox from out his hole
His fur was the colour of a starless night
His eyes like burning coals

They chased him over the valley
They chased him over the field
They chased him down to the riverbank
But never would he yield

He's jumped into the water
And he's swum to the other side
He's laughed so loud that the greenwood
  shook
Then he's turned to the huntsmen and
  cried

"Ride on, my gallant huntsmen
When must I come again?
Oh never shall you want a fox
To chase along the plain

"And when your need is greatest
Just call upon my name
And I will come and you shall have
The best of sport and game."

All the men looked up in wonder
All the hounds ran back to hide
For the fox had changed to the Devil
  himself
Where he stood at the other side

And men and hounds and horses
Went flying back to town
And hard on their heels came the little
  black fox
A-laughing as he ran

"Ride on, my gallant huntsmen
When must I come again?
Oh never shall you want a fox
To chase along the plain."

ANSTRUTHER, THE EAST NEUK, SCOTLAND 1889.

THE GREAT·SELCHIE OF·SULE·SKERRY
© JANE YOLEN AND CHARLES VESS.

TWO MILES OF SMA' LINES EVERY DAY TO BE BAITED AND BARROWED TO HER FATHER'S BOAT. NO WONDER MAIRI MACDONALD WANTED SOMETHING MORE IN HER LIFE.

HE STAYED FOR FIVE MONTHS, AND FOR FIVE MONTHS MAIRI WAS CONTENT. BUT ONE MORNING...

WHERE IS THAT LAD? IT'S TIME WE WERE OFF TO THE BOAT.

GONE. DROONED. I CANNA' BEAR IT, DA.

WEEL, IT WASN' LIKE HE WAS ONE O' US, MAIRI. NOT AN ANSTER LAD, FOR A' HE WAS GUD AT THE LINES.

HE'S TAKEN MY HEART, DA. THERE'S NAUGHT MORE TO KEEP ME HERE.

"WHERE CAN YOU GO? YER A FISHER LASSIE. HERE'S YER HOME."

BUT MAIRI HAD ALREADY THOUGHT OF THAT. SHE WOULD FOLLOW THE FLEETS AND BECOME A HERRIN' LASSIE, GUTTING AND PACKING HERRING IN THE SHEDS. IT WASN'T JUST THAT SHE DESPAIRED OF HER LOST LOVE. THERE WAS SOMETHING ELSE: A CHILD IN HER BELLY. SHE COULD NOT TELL HER FATHER THAT.

NEARLY 6,000 SCOTS GIRLS, HIRED BY CURERS, WENT FROM FISHING TOWN TO FISHING TOWN ALONG THE COASTS. SOME LIVED IN LODGINGS BUT MOST LIVED IN SMALL ON-SHORE HUTS, SLEEPING THREE TO A BED. BUT STILL, FOR MOST IT WAS THE FIRST TIME THEY HAD EARNED MONEY TO KEEP FOR THEMSELVES.

'TIS HARD WARK, BUT IT SEEMS TO AGREE WI' YOU, MAIRI. YOU'VE PUT ON WEIGHT. ME, I'M ALL SKIN AND BONES.

THAT'S THE LOT. WE'VE TIME FOR SOME TEA AND KNITTIN'.

THEN ANE AROSE AT HER BEDFOOT, AND A GRIMLY GUEST I'M SURE TWAS HE, SAYING "HERE AM I, THY BAIRN'S FATHER, ALTHOUGH I BE NOT COMLIE."

YOU'RE DEAD! DROONED! STAY AWAY.

NOT DROONED. YOU CANNA DROON A SELCHIE.

"I AM A MAN UPON THE LAND, I AM A SELCHIE IN THE SEA. AND WHEN I'M FAR FRAE EV'RY STRAND, MY DWELLIN' IS IN SULE SKERRY."

GIVE ME THE CHILD, MAIRI MACDONALD. YOU CANNA RAISE HIM ALANE. IT WOULD SHAME YOU. GO HOME AND MAKE A GOOD MARRIAGE WITH AN ANSTER BOY.

HE WILL HAVE MANY FISH IN HIS NETS. I WILL ASSURE IT.

AND HE HAS TAKEN A PURSE O' GOLD, AND HE HAS PUT IT ON HER KNEE, SAYING "GIE TAE ME MY LITTLE YOUNG SON, AND TAK YE UP THE NOURRICE FEE."

I'M NO FOR ANSTER.

THE GREAT SELCHIE OF SULE SKERRY

In Norway there sits a maid:
"Bye-loo, my baby," she begins,
"Little know I my child's father
Or if land or sea he's living in."

Then there arose at her bed feet,
And a grumly guest I'm sure it was he
Saying, "Here am I, thy child's father,
Albeit I am not comely.

"I am a man upon the land,
I am a selchie in the sea,
And when I am in my own country,
My dwelling is in Sule Skerry."

Then he hath taken a purse of gold,
He hath put it upon her knee,
Saying, "Give to me my little wee son,
And take thee up thy nurse's fee.

"And it shall come on a summer's day,
When the sun shines hot on every stone,
That I shall take my little wee son,
And I'll teach him for to swim in the
    foam.

"And you will marry a gunner good,
And a proud good gunner I'm sure
    he'll be.
And he'll go out on a May morning
And he'll kill both my wee son and
    me."

And she did marry a gunner good,
And a proud good gunner, I'm sure it
    was he;
And the very first shot that e'er he did
    shoot
He killed both the son and the great
    selchie.

In Norway there sits a maid:
"Bye-loo, my baby," she begins,
"Little know I my child's father
Or if land or sea he's living in."

DISCOGRAPHY NOTES

Compiled by Ken Roseman

"Alison Gross"
Steeleye Span: *Parcel of Rogues* (Shanachie 79045; U.K.—BGO BGOCD 323)
Steeleye Span: *Gone to Australia* (On Tour 1975–1984) (Raven RVCD 123) Australian release of live tracks culled from Australian concerts
Lizzie Higgins: *What a Voice* (Lismor LIFC 7004)

"Barbara Allen"
Norma Waterson: *Bright Shiny Morning* (Topic TSCD 520)
Louis Killen: *The Rose in June* (The Old and New Tradition)
Dave Webber and Ani Fentiman: *Constant Lovers* (The Old and New Tradition)
Hilary James: *Love Lust & Loss* (Acoustics Records CDAC 029)
Joan Baez: *Joan Baez, Vol. II* (Vanguard 2907-2)
Emmylou Harris: *Songcatcher Music from and Inspired by the Motion Picture* (Vanguard/Combustion Music 79586-2)
Emmy Rossum: *Songcatcher Music from and Inspired by the Motion Picture*
Shirley Collins: *The Power of the True Love Knot* (Fledg'ling FLED 3028)
Betty Smith: *Both Sides Then & Now* (Bluff Mountain Music BMM 003)
De Danann: *Selected Jigs, Reels, & Songs* (Shanachie 79001)
Also recorded by: Pete Seeger, Jean Redpath, Kay Justice, Ross Kennedy & Archie McAllister, and many others

"The Daemon Lover" (aka "The Demon Lover" or "The House Carpenter")
Natalie Merchant: *The House Carpenter's Daughter* (Myth America MA-1026)
Steeleye Span: *Commoner's Crown* (BGO BGOCD 315)
Ewan MacColl and A. L. Lloyd: *English and Scottish Popular Ballads, Vol. IV* (Riverside 627)
Joan Baez: *Joan Baez in Concert, Part I* (Vanguard 2122-2)

Sweeney's Men: *Sweeney's Men/The Tracks of Sweeney* (double album CD reissue of LPs; Essential ESM CD 435)

Lisa Moscatiello: *Innocent When You Dream* (Happy Cactus HC001)

Mr. Fox: *Mr. Fox/The Gypsy* (double album CD reissue of LPs; Essential ESM CD 433)

Jacqui McShee's Pentangle: *At the Little Theatre* (Park PRKCD 53)

Jacqui McShee's Pentangle: *Passe Avant* (Park PRKCD 046)

Tim O'Brien: *Two Journeys* (Howdy Skies Records HS 1004)

A. L. Lloyd: *Classic A. L. Lloyd* (Fellside FECD 98)

"The False Knight on the Road"

Steeleye Span: *Please to See the King* (Shanachie 79075; U.K.—Crest 005)

Maddy Prior and Tim Hart: *Summer Solstice* (Shanachie 79046)

Steeleye Span: *Live at Last* (BGO BGOCD 342)

"The Galtee Farmer"

Steeleye Span: *Commoner's Crown* (BGO BGOCD 315)

Irish Tinker Singers-2: *When I Was in Horseback* (FTX 167)

"The Great Selchie of Sule Skerry" (note that this ballad appears with many different title variations, such as **"The Grey Selchie"**)

Maddy Prior: *Ravenchild* (Park PRKCD 49)

Solas: *The Words That Remain* (Shanachie 78023)

Jean Redpath: *Jean Redpath* (Philo PH 2015)

"King Henry"

Steeleye Span: *Present* (Park PRKCD 64)

Steeleye Span: *Below the Salt* (Shanachie 79039;U.K.—BGO, BGOCD 324)

Martin Carthy: *Sweet Wivelsfield* (Rounder 3020)

"Sovay"

Polly Bolton, John Shepherd, Steve Dunachie: *Woodbine and Ivy* (self-issued: Oak Barn Centre, Clee St. Margaret, Craven Arms, Shropshire SY7 9DT, England)

Pentangle: *Sweet Child* (Essential ESM CD 354 or Castle Music America 633)

Brass Monkey: *The Complete Brass Monkey* (Topic TSCD 467)

Martin Carthy and Dave Swarbrick: *Life and Limb* (Green Linnet 3052)

A. L. Lloyd: *Classic A. L. Lloyd* (Fellside FECD 98)

Martin Carthy: *The Carthy Chronicles* (Free Reed FRQCD-60)

"Tam-Lin"

Mike Waterson: *Mike Waterson* (Topic 12TS 332)

Fairport Convention: *Liege and Lief* (A&M CD 4257)

Fairport Convention: *Cropredy 2002 Another Gig Another Palindrome* (Woodworm WR2CD 039)

Steeleye Span: *Tonight's the Night Live* (Shanachie 79080)

The Mrs. Ackroyd Band: *Guns and Roses* (Mrs. Ackroyd Records DOG 010)

Pyewackett: *The Man in the Moon Drinks Claret* (MW Records MW CD 4007)

Pete Morton: *Frivolous Love* (Philo PHIL 1122, cassette)

Broadside Electric: *Amplificata* (Clever Sheep CS-1703C)
A. L. Lloyd: *Classic A. L. Lloyd* (Fellside FECD 98)
Frankie Armstrong: *Ballads* (Fellside FECD 110)

"Thomas the Rhymer"
Steeleye Span: *Present: The Very Best of Steeleye Span* (Park PRKCD 64)
Steeleye Span: *Now We Are Six* (Shanachie 79060; U.K.—BGO BGOCD 157)
Robin Williamson: *Five Celtic Tales of Enchantment* (Robin Williamson Productions; cassette only)

"Twa Corbies"
Maddy Prior: *Year* (Park PRKCD 20)
Steeleye Span: *Hark! The Village Wait!* (Shanachie 79052)
Steeleye Span: *Time* (Shanachie 79099)
Ray & Archie Fisher: *New Electric Muse* (Essential ESB CD-416)
Old Blind Dogs: *Close to the Bone* (KRL/Lochshore CDLDL 1209)
Boiled in Lead: *Old Lead* (Omnium OMM 2001)
Robin & Barry Dransfield: *Up to Now: A History of Robin & Barry Dransfield* (Free Reed FRDCD 18)

Source Singer Compilations

Most of the recordings cited above were made by contemporary performers. Some readers may want to investigate CDs featuring "source singers." We list a few here to satisfy that interest.

Classic Ballads of Britain and Ireland, Volume 1 (Rounder 1161-1775-2) (CD includes "The False Knight Upon the Road," "Lord Thomas and Fair Ellen or Fair Annet," and "Barbara Allen." Booklet with detailed information on the ballads included also.)

The Muckle Sangs, Classic Scots Ballads (Greentrax CD TRAX 9005) (includes "The False Knight on the Road," "Tam-Lin," and "Lord Thomas and Fair Ellen")

Anglo-American Ballads, Volume 1 (Rounder 1511) (includes "The House Carpenter," and "Barbara Allen")

Anglo-American Ballads, Volume 2 (Rounder 1516) (includes "Lord Thomas and Fair Ellender")

Versions and Variants of Barbara Allen (The Library of Congress Archive of Folk Culture AFS L54; cassette only)

Performer Notes

FRANKIE ARMSTRONG: Ms. Armstrong specializes in a cappella renditions of traditional and contemporary songs. Songs commenting on contemporary problems are also featured in her repertoire.

JOAN BAEZ: Joan Baez is probably as well known for her social activism as her music. In a career spanning four decades, Ms. Baez has done everything from traditional ballads to protest songs and even pop and country material.

BOILED IN LEAD: Minneapolis-based Boiled in Lead have purveyed their own special brand of Celtic punk and world thrash for almost twenty years! Boiled in Lead crashed into the "fantasy" scene with the CD *Songs from the Gypsy* (Omnium OMM 2013), a collection of songs inspired by Steven Brust and Megan Lindholm's novel *The Gypsy* (Tor Books).

POLLY BOLTON: Polly Bolton brings a bright, jazzy sophistication to her interpretations of traditional songs. Her superb collection of traditional ballads, *Woodbine & Ivy,* has finally been released on CD.

BRASS MONKEY: In the early 1980s, Martin Carthy and John Kirkpatrick (vocals, anglo concertina, button accordion, melodeon) decided to form a very different kind of folk/folk-rock band: entirely acoustic with a rhythm section consisting of a percussionist and trombonist. The trombonist played the bass parts. The band was called Brass Monkey, and joining Carthy and Kirkpatrick were: Howard Evans (trumpet, flügelhorn, vocals), Martin Brinsford (saxophone, harmonium, percussion), Roger Williams (trombone on first album), and Richard Cheetham (trombone on second album). Brass Monkey regrouped in the 1990s and released the CDs *Sound & Rumour* in 1998 and *Going & Staying* in 2001.

MARTIN CARTHY: Singer-guitarist Martin Carthy has been active in the English folk scene for almost forty years. He's played with Steeleye Span, The Albion Country Band, Band of Hope, Brass Monkey, and Blue Murder (Blue Murder is an a cappella "supergroup" featuring members of The Watersons and Swan Arcade). In the 1960s, Carthy was in a pioneering duo with fiddler Dave Swarbrick; the duo reunited in the early 1990s. Martin Carthy was also a member of the famed Yorkshire a cappella group, The Watersons. Carthy teamed up with wife, Norma Waterson, and daughter, Eliza Carthy, to form Waterson:Carthy in the late 1990s. All periods of Martin Carthy's career are documented in *The Carthy Chronicles,* a four-CD box set released by Free Reed.

SHIRLEY COLLINS: Shirley Collins is an influential English folksinger whose career has spanned almost fifty years. She recorded with the brilliant guitarist Davey Graham, as a duo with her sister Dolly, and with the Albion Dance Band (among others). *Within Sound* (Fledg'ling, U.K.) is a four-CD box set giving a great overview of Collins's career.

DE DANANN: Although many singers and instrumentalists have passed through De Danann's ranks, Frankie Gavin (fiddle and whistle master) and Alec Finn (bouzouki and rhythm guitar wizard) have remained as the band's core and kept the group going for around twenty-five years. Gavin and Finn always surrounded themselves with the finest singers and musicians; among those who can claim De Danann stints on their resumes are: Dolores Kean (vocals), Mary Black (vocals), Maura O'Connell (vocals), Martin O'Connor (accordion), Jackie Daly (accordion), and Brendan Reagan (guitar, mandolin).

ROBIN AND BARRY DRANSFIELD: Natives of Harrogate, Yorkshire, England, the brothers Robin Dransfield (vocals, guitar) and Barry Dransfield (vocals, fiddle, dulcimer, cello, guitar) released a series of fine LPs through the 1970s. Some of those recordings are now out of print, but the comprehensive two-CD box set *Up to Now: A History of Robin & Barry Dransfield* (Free Reed FRDCD 18) includes tracks culled from those now hard-to-find albums. I'd also recommend seeking out the two excellent solo CDs Barry Dransfield released in the 1990s: *Be Your Own Man* (Rhiannon RHYD 5003, 1994) and *Wings of the Sphinx* (Rhiannon RHYD 5010, 1996).

FAIRPORT CONVENTION: Fairport Convention can be credited with creating the genre of British folk-rock. They were the first band to fuse the electricity of rock 'n' roll with traditional melodies and rhythms. Over the years many members have come and gone, but still Fairport Convention carries on. The band celebrated its thirty-fifth anniversary in 2002!!

RAY AND ARCHIE FISHER: The Fisher family (which includes sister Cilla) of Scotland have worked solo and in numerous combinations over the years.

HILARY JAMES: An eclectic English singer with a repertoire covering folk, blues, jazz, and pop, Ms. James has recorded three solo CDs: *Burning Sun, Love Lust & Loss,* and *Bluesy*. All three recordings were released on the Acoustics Records label.

NATALIE MERCHANT: Ms. Merchant reached her first fame as songwriter and lead vocalist with the Jamestown, New York–based folk-rock band 10,000 Maniacs. The 10,000 Maniacs' songs and Merchant's vocal style always showed strong American and British folk influences. Since leaving 10,000 Maniacs, Merchant recorded several pop albums, but for her 2003 release *The House Carpenter's Daughter* she decided to concentrate on folk-oriented material.

MR. FOX: This Yorkshire quartet was one of the earliest English folk-rock bands. Their distinctive repertoire contained a number of songs inspired by spooky Yorkshire myths and tales. Founding member Bob Pegg went on to a form a duo with Nick Strutt; they recorded two albums, one of which was the wonderful fantasy-oriented set *The Shipbuilder*. After that Pegg did a solo project, *Ancient Maps,* and in 1996 released *The Last Wolf*.

PETE MORTON: Pete Morton, of Leicester, England, brings a punk rock intensity to his interpretations of traditional ballads. He also writes and performs original songs that eloquently address current political issues.

LISA MOSCATIELLO: Lisa Moscatiello is a gifted Maryland-based singer who received great notices during her several years with the British-styled folk-rock band The New St. George. *Innocent When You Dream,* Moscatiello's first solo album, was released in 1996.

TIM O'BRIEN: Tim O'Brien is a supremely multitalented fellow: an ace singer, songwriter, and instrumentalist (fiddle, mandolin, guitar). He spent ten years with the popular bluegrass band Hot Rize; now he concentrates on solo projects. Several years ago

O'Brien launched The Crossing, a floating collaboration that has included Irish and American musicians.

OLD BLIND DOGS: This clever Scottish folk band funks up their arrangements of traditional ballads and tunes by blending electric bass and various kinds of hand drums with the more conventional fiddle, guitar, banjo, and mandolin. Old Blind Dogs also feature full, precise, four-part vocal harmonies.

PENTANGLE: "Folk baroque" (a fascinating blend of folk, jazz, baroque, blues, and "classical" influences) got its start with guitarist Davey Graham. But the band Pentangle (Jacqui McShee, Bert Jansch, John Renbourn, Danny Thompson, Terry Cox) took that style to its greatest prominence. Vocalist McShee now works with a band called Jacqui McShee's Pentangle, who play a more electric version of "folk baroque."

MADDY PRIOR: Famed for her soaring soprano, Maddy Prior has been Steeleye Span's lead singer for most of their three-decade-plus history. Prior also developed a parallel solo career performing original and traditional material. She also recorded two superb albums with June Tabor as the Silly Sisters.

PYEWACKETT: This English band is no longer active, but they released a brief series of fascinating albums in the 1980s, the best of which was *The Man in the Moon Drinks Claret* which is now available on CD from MW Records. Pyewackett played a brilliant fusion of English roots, "early music," jazz, rock, and '30s pop.

SOLAS: Solas is an Irish-American folk/fusion band based around the instrumental prowess of Seamus Egan (flute, whistles, uilleann pipes, guitar, bodhran) and Winifred Horan (fiddle). Karan Casey was their first lead vocalist.

STEELEYE SPAN: Continually active since 1969 (with a few breaks), Steeleye Span are one of the seminal British folk-rock bands. They're best known for dramatic arrangements of traditional ballads featuring precise multipart vocal harmonies over full electric backing. Ballads with fantastic themes are an important part of their repertoire.

SWEENEY'S MEN: Although they broke up in 1969, Sweeney's Men can lay claim to being one of Ireland's art-folk bands: groups that emphasized instrumental virtuosity and performed songs outside of the standard pub sing-along repertoire.

THE MRS. ACKROYD BAND: To know about The Mrs. Ackroyd Band, you must first learn about Les Barker. This multitalented and sharp fellow is a poet, bandleader, brilliant songwriter, and one-man folk equivalent of Monty Python. Barker's parodies of well-known folk ballads (often complete with satiric political references) have been regaling English fans for years. The Mrs. Ackroyd Band is an occasional touring and recording unit assembled by Mr. Barker.

ROBIN WILLIAMSON: Robin Williamson was a founding member of the Incredible String Band. Since that group split up, Williamson has performed solo and with other musicians, and has recorded story recitations as well as traditional and original songs.

Further Resources

The following magazines have information about contemporary folk, folk-rock, and related music:

Sing Out!, http://www.singout.org
Folk Roots, http://www.frootsmag.com
Dirty Linen, http://www.dirtylinen.com
Penguin Eggs, http://www.penguineggs.ab.ca
The Living Tradition, http://www.folkmusic.net/

CONTRIBUTORS

In her youth, **Emma Bull** personally helped keep the continent balanced by being born in Southern California and moving to Minneapolis, where she became involved in the IWW (the Interstate Writers' Workshop, aka The Scribblies). Her first novel, *War for the Oaks* (1997), won the Locus Award for Best First Novel. After several more years and novels she moved back west; she now lives in Bisbee, Arizona, where she'd ride the range if she had a pony. She doesn't; but she is working on *Territory,* a fantasy novel about the Old West. Besides her novels, Emma has written screenplays, short stories, and a children's book. In her copious spare time she is one-half of the folk duo Flash Girls, along with Lorraine Garland.

Charles de Lint is a full-time writer and musician who presently makes his home in Ottawa, Canada, with his wife, MaryAnn Harris, an artist and musician. Among his most recent books are *The Onion Girl, Medicine Road,* and *Spirits in the Wires.* Other recent publications include the collections *Waifs & Strays* and *Tapping the Dream Tree,* and *A Circle of Cats,* a picture book illustrated by Charles Vess. In 2001, he won the World Fantasy Award for his collection *Moonlight and Vines.* His Web site is at www.charlesdelint.com.

Neil Gaiman is listed in the *Dictionary of Literary Biography* as one of the top-ten living "post-modern" writers. His 2001 novel, *American Gods,* won the Hugo, Nebula, Bram Stoker, SFX, and Locus awards. His first, *Good Omens* (1990), coauthored with Terry Pratchett, was "a very funny novel about how the world is going to end and we're all going to die." Between 1990 and 1994, Gaiman was the co-creator and sole writer of *Sandman,* a landmark monthly comic book that became DC's bestselling title. Among its dozens of awards was the World Fantasy Award for Best Short Story for *Sandman* #19 (art by Charles Vess), making it the first comic book to win a literary award.

Among Gaiman's other works are *Coraline* (2002), a novel for children, and *Stardust* (1998), a prose novel in four parts, with illustrations by Charles Vess.

Emmy-nominated actress and published playwright **Elaine Lee** is best known as the writer of *Vamps* (DC/Vertigo) and *Starstruck* (Heavy Metal, Marvel, Dark Horse). Some of her other comics work includes *Prince Valiant* and *The Transmutation of Ike Garuda* (Marvel); *Ragman: Cry of the Dead* (DC Comics); *Brainbanx* (DC/Helix); *The Galactic Girl Guides* (Comico); *Indiana Jones and the Spear of Destiny* (Dark Horse); and two volumes of erotic science fiction stories, *Skin Tight Orbit* (NBM). With her comedienne sister, Susan Norfleet, she scripted episodes for the animated series *Troll Tales*. Under the name Georgia Sullivan, Elaine and Susan have just completed a humorous self-help book, *Porch Dogs*; check it out at www.porchdogs.com.

Sharyn McCrumb lives and writes in the Virginia Blue Ridge, and is best known for her Appalachian Ballad novels, including *New York Times* bestsellers *She Walks These Hills* and *The Rosewood Casket;* also *The Ballad of Frankie Silver* and *The Songcatcher*. She is the recipient of numerous awards and honors, and her books have been translated into a dozen languages. Her novel *St. Dale,* forthcoming in February 2005, is a mixture of NASCAR and *The Canterbury Tales*.

As half of a noted folk duo with his wife, Eileen, **Graham Pratt** has performed throughout the British Isles. Their act focuses on unaccompanied harmony as well as Eileen's voice accompanied by Graham's guitar, harmonium, keyboard, and concertina. Their performance also features Graham's songwriting; songs like "The Minstrel," "The Black Fox," "The Bundling Song," "Kerry Is No More," and "We Live We Love" have been taken up by other singers and absorbed into the "tradition." Their CD *Borders of the Ocean* was released in 1997. Earlier vinyl albums have been rereleased on CD, including the compilation album *Early Birds* and the album *Bandstand* (with the four-part group Regal Slip).

Ken Roseman is a music journalist who's been covering progressive Anglo-European folk/roots music for over twenty-five years. He's also a comics and fantasy enthusiast who deeply enjoys the works of J. R. R. Tolkien, Neil Gaiman, Robert Crumb, Harvey Pekar, and Alan Moore. Ken has long dreamed of a project that would combine his interests in music, fantasy, and comics, and is therefore very pleased to be involved with the *Ballads* project.

Delia Sherman's short stories have appeared in the *Magazine of Science Fiction & Fantasy* and in numerous anthologies. Her novels are *Through a Brazen Mirror* (1989) and *The Porcelain Dove* (1993), which won the Mythopoeic Fantasy Award, and, with fellow fantasist and partner Ellen Kushner, *The Fall of the Kings* (2002). She has coedited anthologies with Ellen Kushner and Terri Windling and is currently working on an anthology of "interstitial fiction" with Gavin Grant. She is a consulting editor for Tor Books and president of the Interstitial Arts Foundation. She likes cafés for writing (they bring you things to eat and the phone's never for you) and trains and airplanes for reading. She shares a 1910 farmhouse in the wilds of Cambridge, Massachusetts, with Ellen Kushner and many, many papers and books.

Jeff Smith was born and raised in the American Midwest, and learned about cartooning from comic strips, comic books, and cartoons on TV. While most adults consider cartoons to be children's fare, Smith discovered early on that no topic of human experience—from the introspection of *Peanuts* or the politics of *Doonesbury* to the lyricism of *Pogo*—was outside the range of comics. After four years of drawing comic strips for Ohio State's student newspaper, from 1982 to 1986, Smith cofounded the Character Builders animation studio. Then, in 1991, he launched the comic book *Bone.* Currently published in thirteen languages around the world, in 1998 *Bone* was given the Eisner Award for Best Writer/Artist–Humor, as well as the 1998 Harvey Award for Best Cartoonist, Italy's Yellow Kid Award for Best Author, Spain's Premio Expocomic for Best Foreign Comic, and Finland's Lempi International for Best International Cartoonist.

Lee Smith is the author of nine novels, including *Oral History, Saving Grace, The Devil's Dream,* and *Fair and Tender Ladies,* as well as three collections of stories including *News of the Spirit.* Her latest novel, *The Last Girls,* was a *New York Times* bestseller as well as cowinner of the Southern Book Critics Circle Award. She is a retired professor of English at North Carolina State University, and in 1999 received an Academy Award in Fiction from the American Academy of Arts and Letters.

Midori Snyder has published numerous fantasy novels in the United States and Europe, as well as short stories and books for young adults. Her most recent novel, *The Innamorati,* which draws upon upon Italian and early Roman mythology and commedia dell'arte theater, was critically acclaimed in both the United States and Italy, and won the Mythopoeic Award for Best Adult Fantasy Novel of 2000. In addition to writing, Ms. Snyder is the managing editor for the Interstitial Arts Foundation's Web site.

Widely regarded as the preeminent American editor of fantasy, **Terri Windling** is the winner of multiple World Fantasy Awards for her editorial work. Her novel *The Wood Wife* (1996) won the Mythopoeic Fantasy Award. She is also the creator of the shared-world Bordertown series and the editor of many notable anthologies; among the most recent of these is *The Green Man: Tales of the Mythic Forest,* coedited with Ellen Datlow and illustrated by Charles Vess.

Jane Yolen, called the "Hans Christian Andersen of America" by *Newsweek* and the "Aesop of the twentieth century" by the *New York Times* (anyone notice it's the twenty-first century now?), has written over 250 books for children, young adults, and adults. She is a poet as well, and has written lyrics for the bands Boiled in Lead and Folk Underground, as well as for folk singers like Lui Collins. She has won two Nebulas, a World Fantasy Award, two Christopher Medals, and three Mythopoeic Awards. She also has been awarded four honorary doctorates from colleges for her body of written work, which likely makes her Dr. Dr. Dr. Dr. Yolen.

Charles Vess was born in 1951 in Lynchburg, Virginia, and has been drawing since he could hold a crayon. He has been featured in several gallery and museum exhibitions across the nation, including the first major exhibition of Science Fiction and Fantasy Art (New Britain Museum of American Art, 1980) and "Dreamweavers" (William King Regional Arts Center, 1994–95).

In 1991, Charles shared the prestigious World Fantasy Award for Best Short Story with Neil Gaiman for their collaboration on *Sandman* #19—the first and only time a comic book has held this honor. In the summer of 1997, Charles won the Will Eisner Comic Industry Award for Best Penciler/Inker for his work on *The Book of Ballads and Sagas* as well as *Sandman* #75. Soon after, Charles finished the last of 175 paintings for *Stardust,* a novel written by Neil Gaiman, for which he was given the 1999 World Fantasy Award as Best Artist.

In 2002, Charles won a second Will Eisner Award, this time as Best Painter for his work on *Rose,* a 130-page epic fantasy saga written by Jeff Smith. The year continued to be busy for Charles with the publication of *Seven Wild Sisters* and *The Green Man: Tales from the Mythic Forest,* both utilizing cover art and interior black-and-white illustrations by the artist, and both making the 2003 American Library Association's list for Best Books for Young Adults! By the end of the year he had completed twenty-eight paintings for his first children's picture book, *A Circle of Cats,* done in collaboration with writer Charles de Lint. This cover art won the Gold Award for Best Book Art in the 10th annual "Spectrum: The Best in Contemporary Fantastic Art" even before it was officially published. A new edition of *Peter Pan* featuring a cover and over thirty black-and-white interior illustrations by Vess was released in 2003. Vess-illustrated projects published in 2004 include another collaboration with de Lint, *Medicine Road,* and a YA anthology, *The Faery Reel.*

Among Vess's current projects are drawings for several new books, including an illustrated edition of George R. R. Martin's *A Storm of Swords* and the 20th anniversary edition of Charles de Lint's *Moonheart.* Charles Vess's Web site is at www.greenmanpress.com.